A novel

THE BROKEN Rose

BELLE

PAGE PUBLISHING, INC.
New York, NY

First originally published by Page Publishing, Inc. 2018

ISBN 978-1-64082-032-6 (Paperback)
ISBN 978-1-64082-033-3 (Digital)

Printed in the United States of America

Emma was robbed of her innocence, and she was forced
to be naughty; but she loved her revenge . . .

Acknowledgments

Thanks to the women who shared their life experiences of struggle with me. It is their stories that helped me to create this novel. The horrors they suffered have been swept under the rug and kept out of view in their innermost secret places. Their childhood tragedies and pain were kept as personal secrets. No one wanted to talk about it or hear about it. In school, they appeared to be just like other normal girls. Unknown to many, these brave individuals were targeted as sexual prey by community sexual predators. Therefore, they were physically and emotional abused as children.

These women presented and bared little-known facts of how they felt being victimized by their family members and sometimes friends of the family. This experience forced many of them to live a double life. Many of these girls became addicted to sex. Some became alcoholics and substance abusers to soothe away their pain and embarrassment. Most of these women carried a lifetime of guilt and suffering for the indignities of the past. Oftentimes, these women transferred their pain from these childhood violations into their present life, without being aware of how much damage they have suffered both physically and mentally.

The innocent girls in this novel shared with me their life of sexual captivity and trauma. These hidden violations have directly affected their lives today.

This novel is loosely based on their experiences in cruelty and manipulations. I am grateful to God for using me to create works that will touch lives and make a difference for many generations.

The Lord is the source of my very existence. Daily I pray and thank God for life, health, and strength. Most of all, I am grateful for the many lives I have crossed along my life's journey. My careers have crossed many different sectors, and it has enriched the lives of countless people, young and old, around the nation.

A special thanks to my family: Dan and Willie B. Dunnigan, Aunt Beatrice Robinson, Delores and Paul Perry, Tommy Davis and family, Snap, Dan III, Andrew Bowie, Patricia Juliet, da'Vronia, Eddie, da'Vette, TerVette, Tatiana, Nastajjia, Brandon, Kierra, Narcharzeke, Roderick, Jordan, London, Jackson, Zaria. Thank you for your support.

Thank God for my parents. This supportive union gave me strength to dream beyond our environment. Music became my best friend at the age of nine. Both my parents created a shelter for many abused females. This couple dedicated their lives to helping others. Thankfully, they passed this trait of concern to me and, in turn, to my family.

Traveling has given me a deeper knowledge of society and how to acknowledge and embrace other cultures, which makes me very happy.

I am grateful to my mentee for sharing their journey with me. I learned a long time ago how to learn from other people's shared experiences. I have been fortunate enough to have a few wise elders take me under their wings. These wise businessmen, businesswomen, and community leaders have mentored me. Some invested in my business and gave me inside information not readily available for future generations. This great journey has helped shape my success as an entrepreneur and business owner.

Introduction

A rose symbolizes love, faith, honor, beauty, balance, promise, new beginnings, and timelessness. "Sharp thorns produce delicate roses," (Ovid). The unique aroma, beauty, and sensitivity of the rose lure a person into a natural place of beauty. The newborn baby girl is a tiny bud growing from her father's seed. The baby girl develops into a sweet rose. She symbolizes the goodness and beauty of love. Imagine the beauty of its many colors of red, yellow. and a kaleidoscope with the spectrum of the rainbow.

I wanted to pen *The Broken Rose* to bring to life the love and expectation of the precious rose broken by people of trust. I was compelled to connect with Emma's brokenness. She encountered many thorns. Traditionally, the thorns surrounding the rose symbolize sharp pain, thoughtlessness, and loss. The strength inside these females in this novel compelled them to live with fear, doubts and broken dreams. These thrones have torn deep inside their psyche as victims of sexual predators.

These characters will bring to your imagination beautiful roses that were harvested too early. Everyday life nourishes or destroys the girl's petals. Each rose represented a flower with all of its beauty, splendor, majesty, and aroma. Throughout the ages, the female symbolizes the precious rose plant—innocent with great potential.

Emma, Rose, and Bessie represent a rose. Each of the girls is connected to morals or immorality in their environment. Emma is the broken rose; each petal was broken off by a loved one.

This novel presents the silent pain and abuse experienced by many females. The characters drew me to them because the role of the female is often misunderstood or distorted. The gender orientation creates a social myth that plays out in the mind of most males. Every girl is given a name at birth, but she is always considered as her.

I discovered that there are two sides to most women, nice and nasty. Most females' values are established by her family standards. Outside the home, the media, community, school, and church also influence the girls at an early age as to their social role. Children learn from their environment, thereby good and bad is normalized and defined within their immediate environment. The old adage is that girls are made of sugar and spice and everything nice and boys are made of puppy dog tails.

Women in this story shared a worldview that there are two types of female: those who are moral and those who are immoral, and those considered moral were often judgmental of those they considered immoral. Very few women who are considered immoral set out to live an immoral life. They found themselves being forced to do immoral things to survive. The first violation makes the girl an unwilling victim. Surviving the madness can make the victim cold and inerrant. Circumstances and abnormal deviant acts usually force these women to be violated.

The female that is reared with good moral values tends to create her world around those values. This young girl learns her role in society from her first teacher—her mother. Many females discover their dual roles at a very early age. The young girl is taught to be a caregiver. To be a wife and mother is the goal of most females. Early in life, she is taught her role in the media, books, movies, cartoons. The goal is to learn how to take a house and make it a home or be a traditional homemaker as determined by Hollywood.

Generally, the girl may grow up in the home with her mother, father, grandfather, or uncles. The female child is cherished and will become the male's little princess. The male will protect this innocent girl with all his might. The father mirrors the male model that the daughter will look for when she becomes a woman. In this novel, Emma and Bessie are the exceptions.

The evolution of these girls will come full circle. There is a dark side for these girls in their sexual relationships that no one wants to consider or talk about. However, *The Broken Rose* will reveal and bring to light all their hidden secrets.

The sexual predator male seeks out helpless girls to make their sexual fantasies come true. Usually, this male is self-absorbed. When he is a boy, he enjoys hurting animals and people. Many of his aberrant behaviors are ignored or normalized by his family. The violator learns that there are no boundaries. Grooming becomes second nature to this predator. Many modern movies and television shows often describe the predator. Seldom do we see and experience the damage and personal pain of long-suffering by the victim. *The Broken Rose* will give these victims an opportunity to share their pain and suffering as survivors.

Emma

I am writing about this great day in my journal. Today, Grandma is taking me to the Royal Theater. This is the one and only theater for colored folk in this town. This big beautiful movie house has a big stage and screen where the movie is played. There are long red curtains on each side of the screen. We love relaxing inside the cool theater watching the movies in these big padded seats. This is a special treat just for the two of us. The only other movies I have seen were at Michael's house. Michael is a teen that lives in our neighborhood. He has a projector that he uses to show movies to the children in the community. His movies were shown outdoors. He uses the side of his house as the screen. The charge is twenty-five cents admission. We sit in lawn chairs or on the long wooden benches to watch the show. He said this is like going to the drive-in movies. All of the movies are in black and white. Many of the movies were cartoons. A few are Western cowboy movies. I like them okay.

Granny says today is our day. She is giving me a special treat. We ride the bus to town. I sit by the big rear window, the wind is blowing in my face. I have a great feeling of freedom. When we arrive in town, I am skipping happily along in the front of Granny. There are so many big furniture stores along our way to the theater. The furniture seems so elegant. I like using fancy words to describe these expensive rooms of furniture. Granny says we can daydream about the fancy furniture because poor people can't buy this kind of furniture with the money they make from local jobs. This type of furniture is for the aristocrats. It is nice to dream, she said.

Now we are in the real movie theater. The preview starts before the main movies. We see all the news reels. This is one way Negroes got the news. The radio is the other best way we get our information about things happening around the world. Most colored people do not buy the newspapers because they can't read English. Many of the people read and speak Gullah in my neighborhood. This is a language with a mixture of Creole. Most people speaking Gullah talk very fast with a slight accent. This language can be hard to understand.

The other name for this language is Geechee. This language is spoken by African descendants who migrated from the Sea Islands along the coastal regions of South Carolina, Georgia, northeast Florida, and Alabama. I have learned this from one of the senior ladies in my neighborhood. Later we will study about this language in school. Regardless of what language these neighbors speak, everybody wants to know the news in our community.

After you go to the movies, this news will give you bragging rights; you would gladly talk about the news you saw in living colors. I have much to tell when I get home. Today is my birthday. I feel like a big girl now. Soon I will be a teen. Granny says this is the last year for me to enjoy little girl things. Next year I will be an adolescent, but today, it is a special stage of growing up. This date with Granny says I am a big girl. It is just the two of us sharing this once-in-a-lifetime day.

Many grown folks can't read. My granddad can't read. The folk that can't read don't pay the printed news much attention. They will sit and listen to the person reading the paper or magazine and memorize what they heard. The listeners will carry the message by ear. Believe it or not, my granny can read. She was reading the news reel in the movies.

When Granny was working, she would bring the newspapers home from her job and sit on the front porch and read to me and the neighbors. Now that Granny is not working anymore, we get the news much later. The maid saves the newspapers from Granny's old job once a week. The gardener brings the newspapers once a week. Oh well, I like the news here in the movie. Cisco Kid and Superman will be showing next week.

I liked the preview. The music started with "Happy Trails to You." That is the song that Roy Rogers and Dale Evans would sing in all of their movies. Roy Rogers and Dale Evans are the famous cowboys of our times. Dale is a pretty white cowgirl. She has her own horse. I love to see her ride off in the sunset with her husband, Roy Rogers. Her long blonde hair bounces in the wind—this was the last movie in the preview.

Finally, the main movie we heard so much about began to play. We were watching the movie *Imitation of Life*, starring Lana Turner and Susan Kohner. Juanita Moore played the black maid. Mahalia Jackson is featured as the choir director in this movie. The story line gives a glimpse into the life of a colored maid and her light-skinned daughter. This daughter was ashamed of her mother's black skin. These concepts the daughter cherished are deeply rooted in the slave experience.

The daughter in this movie had experienced some special social privileges because of her light skin. The source of the lighter-skinned person originated from the ole master's bloodline. His offspring by a slave black woman usually produced a lighter-skinned child. Many harsh words are spoken to the darker person. Granny calls it interracial discrimination. The light-*skinned person is discriminated against by the darker-skinned people in the African-American community*, Granny said.

I was surprised to see and hear a Negro woman singing in the movies. Granny smiled and said, "That is Mahalia Jackson. I think this lady has the best voice in the world." She says, "Listen, baby, Mahalia Jackson had a very strong voice like none other." I am fascinated with this singer. This Negro woman sounds different from the country Western and rock singers on our radio. Her tone of voice was the clearest I've ever heard. In this movie, she sung "Soon I'll Be

Done with the Troubles of This World." This song makes my granny cry. There is a lot of pain in this movie. Colored folk have suffered, yet they still continue to stick together in bad and good times. I don't understand a lot going on in this movie. It seemed to justify the cruelty of racism Grandma has suffered all her life.

We shared a big bag of popcorn and two cups of water. Today, Grandma brought me chocolate-covered peanuts. What a birthday present this was. This was by far one of the best days of my life. There is a strong bond between the two of us as we enjoyed the movies. There is no fear of Granddad's cursing and abusing us today. We are safe in the movies. I love my granny. She is the only mother to lead and show me the things of life. Every day, my granny shows how much she loves and cares for me.

When we came out of the movie theater, Granny stopped at the curb market. The white lady asked, "Can I help you, Aunty?" Granny smiled and says, "Yes, mam. This young great grand of mine is celebrating her big twelfth birthday with me. I want her to have her first real rose."

This middle-aged white woman walked over to me and asked, "What is your name, girl?" She was so close to me, it frightens me. I said, "My name is Emma."

The lady said, "I only sell my roses in a half dozen or dozen." Granny dropped her head and said, "I don't have the money to buy a half dozen."

She walks over to her rose table. The lady says, "Here, little missy, I am going to give you this special yellow rose." She put one rose in a plastic tube and hands it to me. "Most people say this yellow rose represents special love for a friend. This rose for you is a sign of my friendship."

Granny

I took Emma's hand as we walked to the bus stop. My heart beamed as I looked at my sweet Emma, saying God plucked you from his garden and send you to me. I held her hand as we walked to the bus stop. Emma looked up and said, "God gave me a special granny. I know that you loved me. Granny, it makes me feel safe the way you protect me." My love Emma smiled and asked, "Did God send you from his rose garden in heaven?" This little girl brought tears to my eyes. I kissed her and said, "You are the first person to call me rose." I kneeled before Emma and said, "Well baby I guess God did send me as a Rose." My little Emma, you have filled my life with the fragrance of a sweet rose. What a blessing you are to me. In the midst of all the darkness from Mule's abuse, you are my light of hope." We rode the bus home. I let Emma sit next to the window. That was a sweet ride. The entire world seemed so pretty on that special twelfth birthday.

Emma whispered to me, as I stroked her face, "I don't want our special time to end." "How about a little shopping spree at the new Belk Hudson store? They just opened a new store across town. Later we can go home." she shouted, "Can we? Oh, thank you, Granny I love you. This is my best birthday."

We rode past our bus stop and rode another hour before arriving in front of the store. There were big glass windows surrounding the front of the store. The huge windows were full of pretty fancy clothes on tall skinny white mannequins. I said we could not afford to buy any of those clothes. The fancy clothes were not made in my size. We went inside Belk Hudson. My dear Emma has never been inside a gigantic store before. The place was spacious, pretty, and fancy.

I took my Emma's hand and walked through the first floor. She said the things on the floor were too expensive for us to buy. The elevator was located in the rear of the first floor. We rode the big shining elevator to the third floor.

The third level carried all the household goods. The dishes were so beautiful and nice. I said, "Emma, be careful. Don't touch those dishes. I will not have the money to pay for them. Look but don't touch the tableware. Okay, we can go up to the fifth floor." Up we went. The big elevator soared to the top of Belk's new store in a flash. The door opened; we did not get out. We rode from the top floor to the basement one more time. When the doors opened, we waved and said, "Hello, people, we are flying."

The saleslady waved at us, smiling. Emma pushed the button for the basement and off we went. That was a delight I would never forget.

I told my Emma to enjoy this special day. I looked down at her and said, this remarkable day comes once in a lifetime. Your life will be different as a teen. Granny baby girl is growing up too fast. It seems like it was yesterday that I was feeding you and changing your diapers. Just look at you now. Is this a thrilling day so far? I looked into Emma's eyes and said Mule is nowhere around. It is just the two of us. This is our day. She yelled yes, Granny. I never dream that this would be so much fun. I enjoyed this day baby girl. This is about as close as we can get to flying. Poor folk don't have the money to fly on an airplane. That must be a thrill." We were fascinated with all those shinning new pots and pans. Everything was bright. I declare on this day that Emma's eyes were sparkling like shining starts. Excitement filled the air. I decided to splurge on this special day. It was a surprise, when I said we are going to buy one of these new shining graters. She looked so surprised. She said can we Granny? Smiling I said yes Emma we can. Now we can grate our own cabbage at home.

There were so many big fancy electric mixers. I smiled saying, "This is the kind of mixer I used at Mrs. Cleveland's house. Rich folk can buy these kinds of mixers. We colored folk used our hands to beat our cakes and pies. You can't tell the different once the cake is cooked. Our parents taught us how many strokes we had to do to make our cake perfect."

"There is a magic ingredient we use to make our cake light and fluffy. I will show you the next time I bake a cake. Many people pay me to make wedding cakes. My specialty is the rainbow wedding cake." I made extra money baking. "All of my cooking is done by beating my batter by hand. Mule has a birthday coming up in one month. We can cook his birthday cake together okay. That will be fun."

When we got to the basement it was huge. I told Emma this was a learning trip to the linen department. I wanted her to see the best linen we could not afford, so I could teach her like my mother taught me. First you would go and see the finest linen set and duplicate them with cheaper material with similar patterns found in Kress, Woolworth or the five and ten cent store. I will never forget those special shopping and wishing trips with your grandmother. Emma I remembered those special times oh so well. I am doing what my mother did for me years ago. Times were different we did not have the money I have today. Finally, we saw the linen. I would learn to make my own table cloth years ago. I remember your grandmother come to the big fancy stores and see the pretty linen collection. She would go to the five- and ten-cent store or fabric shop and buy the fancy material. She knew just how much fabric to buy in order to fit the table. My mother knew the different shapes and sizes of each table. She would buy just enough to make the napkins and table cloth. Today we can look, but all these linens are too expensive for us to buy.

Most people thought she bought the linen sets in the store. My mother made clothes for all of us. She specialized in curtains and bedspreads. She taught me everything I know. We couldn't buy a tablecloth in that store. They were too expensive, but we could buy one pretty dish towel to dress up our kitchen.

Well, my sweet Emma I am going to buy this set of dish towel. The pretty bright dish towel seemed like it was made just for our home. I bought the towel. It had red and white roses on each end. I smiled and said to Emma this is exciting. I had never been shopping like that before. The pretty curtains were waving in the wind as a fan blew the air. There were beige, brown, gold, yellow, red, orange, white, and black curtains. Some were short, others were long. Others curtains were sheer. There were many kitchen and bathroom curtains. I told Emma, "We need curtains, we can tell your poppy the price of these curtains. I know he will not pay these prices. We will wait until they are marked down. The best price for us will be on the clearance table. After a few weeks they will send the clearance items here in the basement."

I smiled and told Emma, "Come, my dear let us go. Emma went over to the other big table and said her look Granny all this is on clearance." She smiled and said, "Here we are at the clearance tables." Emma yelled come Granny this side of the basement is filled with so many pretty clothes. I looked. It sadden me to say baby I don't have enough money to buy you any of these clothes. When you become a teacher you can come down to this basement and buy as many clothes as you want to. Sales were all over the floor. I went from one clearance table to the other. I told my sweet girl, "This is where you will always find the best bargains. I found many suits in Belk's other store bargain basement. The last white suit I bought myself came from Belk Hudson's basement. The suit was originally priced at $95. It cost me $19.95.

"Later I shopped at Sally's hat store on the east side. That was where I found a pretty white hat. I paid $5 for it. My white hat really accents my suit. You know, I get many compliments on that outfit every time I wear it. I needed a white bag to go with the outfit for the convention. I found a nice pink-and-white pocketbook. Together they made me look as pretty as the aristocrats in the convention. This is the one time churches from our denomination gather people from around the country. The last day of the convention, the missionary officers marched into the big auditorium. My dear girl, you should have seen your granny. I strode down the aisle like I was a millionaire. That was a great day for me. I felt so special. Our pastor and his wife said I look like a pretty Christian ambassador. It is very special to receive a compliment from the two of them."

I have been the president for the missionary society in our church for thirty years. I feel a glow on my face when I talk about Faith Baptist.

Everybody knows how much I love my church and community.

Granny said, "Come Emma I will buy you this pretty white cotton bra here in the famous Belk's Basement. When your great-aunt Bessie was growing up, I brought a bra that would last her a year. Bessie did not mature as fast as you have. You are growing so fast your bras only last seven or eight months. I am not complaining. It takes a lot of money to keep you in proper clothing." Granny does the best she can. My sweet birthday girl kissed my hand and said thank you for everything, the joy you bring to my life.

I came around in the front of Emma. I kneeled saying, "Be a good student and make me proud. After you finish college and become a teacher, you will have your own money to buy whatever you want to buy.

"Little Emma, you will be the first person in the family to go to college. This will make you independent. It pays to go to college and make a good life for yourself. Your education will make you self-sufficient. You will not have to depend on a man like I do. When you have your own money it makes a different. Don't get me wrong. It is a blessing to have a supportive husband." I got nervous when I looked at the clock in the store. Emma knew I was scared. I said, "Baby our time is running out." I don't want any trouble with our boss man Mr. Mule," Granny said. "He doesn't allow me out after dark." Poppy bragged about his power over his home and farm. I told Emma, "Come baby. I hope we are not in trouble with Poppy."

We have another two hours to get home without causing any trouble.

Quietly, we rode two different buses to get home. We walked from the bus stop playing games. That was a true fun day for me. I am a happy old woman today. It has meant too much to make my great grand daughter happy. Change soon to the day is almost over. The two of us will go back to our lonely routine. I regret that there are no happy sounds in my home. When my husband gets home from work he sucks all the joy out of us. That man of mine is never happy Emma. She looked at me and said I have my own imaginary world to keep me happy when I am alone Granny. I gave my sweet great grand a loving hug and we went to our room. I heard the water running as she seem to enjoy a long birthday bathe. Later I went in and tucked Emma in for the night she was snuggling up with her doll Ann. I do declare it looked like the doll's eyes were sparkling in the dark I told Emma she was so special to me. I gave Emma her birthday kiss good night.

I was so glad that tonight, when we arrived at home, Mule was lying across the bed snoring. I went to the bathroom, took a bath, and slipped into my room. Quietness filled the house. Later I put on my gown and slipped into my bed. I soften my skin with Vaseline. This was a very special day. I prayed a prayer of thanksgiving.

Quietly I slide into bed beside my husband. I wish he would sleep his drunk off tonight and let me rest. I hate the way he makes me feel, as he use my body like an animal. I don't enjoy his demands, but I must obey his every command. Tomorrow we need to talk to Emma about growing into her teens and becoming a young lady. This innocent child knows nothing about adolescent. We must have that special womanhood talk with her. I snuggled up in my cover to relax. I thought Mule was sleeping. Suddenly, he said, "So you had a good day with Emma?" I said, "Yes, Mule, it was a pleasant day."

"All right you made that little gal happy now you must make me happy. I need my icing from my chocolate cake. Baby, you know I love this hot chocolate." "Don't you dare move these jugs when I am enjoying my special chocolate milk, sweet Mattie. Yes, baby, that's it . . . give to your big boss man. Make it good, Mrs. Mattie.

That's right. You know this is your duty to keep me happy like a good wife." Mule was noisier than usual as he took control of my body. On this special night I did not like the loud sexy sounds he made. I was so embarrassed. I wondered why does Mule have to make so much noise as he drank his chocolate milk?

I kept saying my sweet Emma does not need to hear the noises tonight. I whispered sh- Sh- he got mad. I reached over and turn my little radio on loud to drown out the sounds. We have a small television sitting in the corner of the living room. Tonight I wish I could turn it on. We were not allowed to play it after 9:00 p.m. I enjoy watching TV with Emma. That is my happy time in the afternoon. I don't like to watch television with my husband. He cursed a lot at the people on the television.

Tonight, I turned my radio on. Sam Cook was singing on the broadcast. The song "You Send Me", well Mule dose not send me. I am an older woman that knows I am helpless as he sexually abuse and misuse me. Later another song touched me as the song said "a change is going to come", I don't know who made the song, but for me there will never be a change until Mule is dead. These songs are not my favorites.

Catherine

Emma is my best friend in class. We call her Emma, but her real name is Emma Louise. Only her family and friends can call her Rena. We have been friends since the first grade. It is so much fun spending time together. We spend long hours in the library when we finished our assignments. Reading exciting books makes my life happy. These books let us travel to many faraway places. I love make-believe.

I have always been taller than Emma. Now we are in the seventh grade. She wants to be a teacher. I want to be a nurse. I pray we could be roommates in college. It would be like having a sister living in the room with me.

I dream of living in the dormitory with Emma Louise. We will work very hard to be smart professionals. It takes a lot of money to go to college. Our English teacher told me if I keep my grade up, she will help us get a scholarship. Our principal said he sat on the board of director at an all-girls college. He said he would help us get a scholarship to help pay for our tuitions. This aspiration gives us a chance for better lives.

This year we will study harder. We are going to volunteer for extra work in science. When I get my assignment I am going to work hard and finish early. We decided that nothing is more important to us than school. I love learning. Maybe when Emma and I get to college, we can listen to music as long as we like.

It makes me sad that we can only see each other in school. Emma knows my favorite game is dodgeball. I have a big ball, but she can't come to play with me. She is skinnier than me, but I am the fastest when it came to running track. If she could come over, I could probably outrun her.

I can't forget the many good times we had in the gym. When we were in gym, we played badminton, volleyball, tennis, and basketball. The whole class played together. When basketball was taught, Coach Love divided us up into two teams. Emma always shot the highest balls and scored the most points. I love that girl. She is the best shooter on the basketball court. I miss my friend Emma when she is out of school.

We both maintain good grades. She gets upset when I score higher on a test than she does. Our teachers have gotten the news about our friendly competition. Emma says we can travel when we graduate from college. During the summer, we cannot call each other on the phone. It makes me sad that we can only see each in school. Right now, I wish she was here at home with me. Summer is here Emma has no one to play with.

Emma complains that the summer is long and boring. She says she has only one person to play with and have fun. Emma says it gets very hot in their tiny kitchen when she and her Granny is canning for the winter. My classmate said that they only have one big electric fan in the living room. Poor Emma Louise fanned her face when she thought about their hot kitchen. She said we need a fan in Granny's kitchen. The kitchen gets really hot when Granny is cooking and canning during the long hot summer days. I wish Emma could see our garden. Emma says her Granny and Poppy have a garden that makes food to can. My friend brags so much about her Granny and Poppy's garden. They harvest so much food to can for the winter. She made me think about my family working together pulling weeds and chopping. Finally we do the same as Emma's family. We preserve and cann for the long cold winter. My mother said this is a survivor's skill.

I have two brothers to play with me in the dirt and sand. My classmate Emma has no one to have fun with when we are out of school. I bet they have fun laughing and playing in the dirt. Emma and her Granny is very lonesome in the summer. Emma says it is just she and her Granny. She sounds lonely to me. Gloom comes on Emma's face when she talks about the way she feels when her great grand dad gets home. My class mate Emma says she sit on the back porch and sing. That is the only fun she has. Sadly she says she feels so alone when we are out of school for the summer. She is completely isolated.

The children in our class live in a different world from Emma. I notice every time we have fun day at school or any special event and our parent are invited Emma only has her Granny. Emma Granny is so polite she says thanks to the teachers for helping her great granddaughter. It never fails at the end of our school affair, Emma's Granny' mood always change. Sadness comes on her face as they leave the school. Emma said she feels sad when her parents never show up to support her. I heard Mrs. Green says what kind of parents does this child have? Have they ever been to the school? I feel so sad when my friend Emma confines in me. It is always with a sad face she sniffled and says. My parents do not love me; if they did they would come to our school activities like your family. I only have Granny and my doll Ann. School is closing. This is a sad time for Emma and me. We always hug tightly and say I love you. Most of us kids are looking forward to free time to play now that school is out, but for my friend Emma the last day of school is a sad beginning for a long boring summer. Emma Louise has a journal she told me her journal is the only place she can share her feelings thoughts, and rejections. I will never forget our last day of school together. She whispered in my ear and said she has a secret place she can hide her journal. Louise smirked and said Poppy can't read even if he find my journal, so my secrets are safe.

These are the times I can see and feel my granny's pain and disappointments. People call my daddy Pretty Boy. He doesn't want me either. My granny Mattie is Pretty Boy's mother. I often hear my granny say she took me home from the hospital. She told me, "Your no-good mama do not have time for you." There are many scary secrets hidden in the walls of this ole house. When we get home, Grandma always say, "I told you, your mama didn't want you. Going to these activities at school is your mother's job. My son ain't no good either. This makes me feel like I did something wrong. "What kind of daddy is he? Has he ever been to your school?" I dropped my head and said, "No, ma'am." These are the times this house seems cold and dark as I hurried to bed and talked to my doll Ann. My room is small and scary. I feel so intimidated and afraid. Now I am at home, I have to play with Ann; there are no children that can come and play with me. Playing is the best part of my life. All the girls say they can't come to our house because their parents will not put their young daughters in danger around Louise's Poppy after what happened to Bessie. In the midst of all this loneliness is a friend of my great granny. He smiles and tells me I am a good girl.

Jake

Every Friday when Poppy got paid, he got drunk and beat my granny. Their friend Jake would quietly slide in the house. He would always say, "It does not take all that to control your woman." He would wipe her wounds and put menthol on the injury followed by salve on the bruise of torn skin.

My grandma trusted this man. He would help her in the garden on those days my granddaddy was too drunk to weed, chop, or harvest the garden. He was so quiet. My great grandparent loved and trusted him as though he was a member of the family. Everybody called him Bo, but his name was Jake.

Jake lived alone in Shelton's Quarter. Grandma said, "That boy works hard. I call him boy because he grew up with my boy. Don't know why that man never found a wife." Sometimes Jake would say to Grandma, "I never found a woman I want to marry." I didn't know how old he was, but Grandma said he went to school with my daddy. His mother died two years ago, and there was no other family around him. Every day after work, Jake would clean up and come and sit on our front porch. "How are you ladies feeling today? Well, it's a good day to be alive and free," he said, smiling.

Granny would smile and say, "Jake, your mere presence brings peace and protection to this house." He would flash that big smile and say, "I must protect my favorite ladies always. You are the only family I got around here." We would sit on the front porch and wave at the neighbors as they passed by. The neighbors were accustomed to seeing the three of us happy together sitting on the front porch facing the main throughway. Our house was located near the old dirt road.

Jake would always look at me and say, "Children today got it easy. Back in my day, we had to work the farm until harvesttime. We only went to school three months a year. Sometimes we went to school for a couple of months. It was depending on the crop and how ole master felt. The straw boss told us, 'Boys, you all don't need to go to school. When you are strong enough to carry a bucket, it's time for you to go to work here on the farm.'

"Look at this little gal you got here Mrs. Mattie. She can go to school nine months of the year. Listen, little Emma, you are so blessed."

"Yes, sir."

"You got it made. Just eat and sleep is all you got to do. All you have do is do a little house work and help Ms. Mattie in the garden. The two of you keep this home sparkling clean. Sometimes this little gal will help you with the hogs and that's her day."

Most evening we sat outside until eight or nine o' clock. In the summer we sat on the porch until it cooled off. We sat and enjoyed the outside as late as 9:30 p.m. in the summer. The days were shorter in the fall and winter. We would sit in the kitchen when it was cold. Many times Jake would say, "Come here, little woman." Grandma Mattie would reply, "She is not a little woman yet. She is still a young gal." Smiling, he would say, "Yes, ma'am, it won't be long. Both of us know she will be a young woman in a little while.

"Mrs. Mattie you sure got a polite little gal here. Emma has good manners. This girl's ways are just the opposite of her mammy, but she is made up like her mama. It is a shame her mammy don't have time to raise her own child. God will bless you, Mrs. Mattie.

"That's the reason I will always give the two of you what you need. It is good to have a woman of God raising this forsaken child. I don't know what would happen to her if it was not for Mrs. Mattie Power. No, sir. I don't know if nobody else told you, but you are unique. You have raised your children and grandchildren. Now you are raising the great-grand. See, Little Emma, how special you are?"

Every evening Jake would say the same thing: "Come here, Emma, I got something for you. This little gal is our pet, ain't that right, Mrs. Mattie?"

"Yes, you are right, Jake," as Granny smiled. He would pat his thigh and say sit on ole Bo's lap. He always brought Grandma something. Sometimes he would bring her pickled pig's feet, Vienna sausage, or potter meat and crackers. "Here you go, Mrs. Power, I brought you a snack to let you know how special you are to me. He and Granny will sit and talk for hours. He brings Granny a Coke, skins, and some snuff. I get a bag of snacks five days a week.

"Hold on, little woman, I got something for you." He smiled and said, "Emma, I never go to the store without thinking about you. Look in the bag and see what I brought you. It is your favorite Baby Ruth candy, moon pie, potato chips, and a strawberry soda." Each day my treat was different. "You still like them, don't you?"

"You know this is what I like, Mr. Jake."

"Don't call me Mr. Jake. You can call me Bo."

Grandma spitted her snuff out and began to eat her treats. "You know what I love, young man. We are grateful for everything you do around here." Many loud laughs followed as they told jokes to each other.

My Private Horsey

One day Jake said, "You have a private horsey, let's ride little girl. Git up, horsey! Ride your stallion, Ms. Emma. Yeah, ride your own horsey. Slow down, horsey, you are going too fast," Jake said smiling. "Let Miss Emma enjoy her ride." Jake was whipping my horsey. When Grandma got through eating her snack, she nodded off.

Mr. Jake Brown always said, "Mrs. Powers is not a young woman anymore. She works very hard caring for you and Mule. Mrs. Mattie is up at 5:00 a.m. to cook breakfast before her husband goes to work. This good wife packs a big lunch for Mule every day. Then she gets you ready for school. The rest of her day she is cleaning, cooking, and sewing.

"Every evening she has Mule's dinner ready when he gets home. Later she feed the hogs most days. This elderly lady never rest before bed. You know she is awake daily until after 9:00 p.m. So, little Ms. Emma, you see, I am Mrs. Mattie relief person. I am here to give her a little rest taking care of you. Okay, we will have a good time while she rest."

We were singing "She'll Be Coming Round the Mountain When She Comes." I felt something pressing against my back side. I yelled. He smile and said, "It's okay, Emma, you are all right. That's nothing to worry about just relax." I said something stuck me; he smiled and said, "That is just old Bo breaking you into your saddle." I said I don't like it. I hopped up and ran inside. Grandma was still sleep. I wanted my mama. She was nowhere to be seen.

Tonight I feel so alone. Grandma is sleeping as my horsey ride was uncomfortable. Why did he smile when I told him the stick punch me? It is like my pain didn't matter to him. That's not nice. Jake has always been good to us. I made up in my mind I don't want to ride the horsey anymore. Well, I wonder does it really hurt the cowgirls when they are riding on their saddle in the movies? I do like watching the white girl riding her own horse. My hair is short and curly. It won't bounce like the cowgirl's hair. I do feel the wind as I ride my horsey.

I love riding my horsey. Rena and I play make-believe, so I guess it is the same with Mr. Brown. I didn't see a saddle. What did he mean? Jake said he was breaking me into my saddle? Where is my parent? Why can't they be here so they could tell me about the horsey and saddle Jake is talking about?

Now I wish my mama would pop in for a short while. I know my mother's face, her smell, her voice. She will come in stay a day or two. This time I want to tell her about these kinds of things. When my mommy returns, I will do everything for her to like me maybe she would stay with me this time. Even when she is with me, she seemed so far away.

I feel like I am not a part of my mama, even when she is sitting right next to me. I wanted to do everything right maybe she would love me. I never felt warmth from my mother. The last time she was here was a quick out of the blue visit. There was joy in my heart my mama was here with me. She stayed two days, and then she hopped up cursing. A few beers later, she walked out the back door and returned ten months later. Why can't she stay with me?

My daddy is known as Pretty Boy. He would come in with his hair Marcelled, acting like he was in a movie. Granny said that son of mine wears very expensive clothes. He thinks he is a model. My father will walk passed me. He never speaks to me or hugs me. He acts like he doesn't see me. I remembered this day, he said, "Hey, young gal, you are growing a rack like your mammy. She proudly wears those two big jugs on her chest. Oh yeah, I remember that about her dumb ass." I didn't understand what he was telling me, but it didn't sound good.

Whenever I was sad, I would lie down on my bed and cry. I miss my parents. There is no fun and laughter in my house except with Granny and her play son Jake. I felt so all alone many times.

The muddy road is deep in the front of the house. When I look at the deep dark slippery mud holes, it makes the world feels so cold. Whenever Jake sees me crying, he would always wipe away my tears. He was Granny's friend. He said, "Emma, you can count on me. I am solid as a rock. Always take care of your granny." A week went by Jake came at his usual time. He did not ask me to sit on my horsey. Grandma asked, "What's wrong, my baby?"

I said, "I am okay." She wrapped her arms around me and said, "You are my pride and joy, sweet girl." This was different. Granny did not do this often.

This day, Granny and Jake told stories about life in Christian Valley. This is the place where Granny and Jake's mother grew up. I did not know the songs they sang, but these songs sound so good. Theses melodies sooth away my pain and loneness; only joy and comfort filled the air. The third week when Jake came by I had forgotten I was mad with him. He gave me a special present. He said, "I saw this pretty little dog in the store window I had to get it just for you." It was a cute black soft dog. He placed the little puppy in my arms. He said, "You can sleep with this little puppy." My new Ebony had black soft curly hair dog. Instantly, I fell in love with the dog.

Emma

I had my own puppy. Jake asked, "What you are going to name your puppy? I hesitated. I said, "I will name her Ebony." Grandma held my dog for a while. My new puppy seemed to wag her little tail as Granny talked to her. She smiled and said, "That was so thoughtful of you, Jake, to buy this little gal a dog. I love it. She gave me my puppy back and said, "Now you have something else to sleep with you and your doll." Of course Jake brought our favorites. He left early. Ebony and I had a good sleep. I felt so good holding on to my new puppy.

A few days later, the three of us were singing and having fun again. The next few weeks, the stick was not in the saddle. I rode the horsey and enjoyed it. It really was fun. Now I feel very secure on my horsey, but I didn't like all that rocking my horsey did.

One day I asked, "Why do you rock me when I am riding my horsey? It doesn't feel right." Jake said, "It's just my way of smoothing all the bad things away." On this day my horsey kept bouncing me harder and longer. I yelled, "Will you slow down, horsey?" And he did. Smiling, Jake said, "It is your horsey, so you can ride fast or slow okay."

He always gave me my candy bar first. He would say, "Mount up, let's ride Miss Emma." Once I start riding, he would always give me some hard candy to suck on. Smiling he would say, "Lie back, little Emma, savor your candy and enjoy your ride." This night, he said, "There a cinnamon roll in your bag. I bought it for you to eat in the morning." Smiling, Jake said, "I am just like a dad to you, ain't that right? One day you will call me daddy."

His face changed as he said, "That sorry, no-good daddy of yours ain't worth a shit. All he has ever done is lay and play. He has never been responsible for any of his five children. That is why Mrs. Mattie is raising you. This old woman loves you that a fact. Everybody knows that."

What did that mean? "Don't worry, little gal. You will be okay." He left early this night. Jake said, "Ole Bo got to work early in the morning. I see you ladies tomorrow. Call me if you need me Mrs. Mattie. Take good care of our little gal."

One day I asked, "Why I can't sit on your lap, Granny?"
"Well, gal, I am too old to whirl you high and let you have fun. Your face lights up as you enjoy riding your horsey. It makes me happy to see you smile as you get pleasure from that horsey or bicycle ride. God knows I want to buy you your own bicycle, but I don't have the money."

Jake smiled and said, "Your grandma knows I am strong and can let you ride your horsey when you want to gallop or ride rough. Remember, don't let anybody else give you a ride. This is your own personal carriage.

"Here is your bicycle. Sit down and enjoy the ride." This was a slow ride. I was smiling. After a while, I was gliding along eating candy smiling and having fun. The bicycle rides ended when I turned ten years old.

As I got older, my horsey ride became bumpy. Now my horsey bucked a lot. The ride got rough when he moved very fast. "Let's have some fun. This is like the rodeo you see in the movies.

"I need you to learn how to enjoy the journey, little Emma." My horsey was dipping and bobbling this day. "This is a rough ride," I yelled. It felt scary. I was holding on for dear life. He dipped, and I thought I was falling. I yelled, "Will you please slow down, horsey, I am falling." He smiled and said, "I got you, little gal." I was safe in his arms. He smiled and said, "See, you don't ever have to worry, Ole Bo got you. You can't fall."

I wonder what it would feel like for Granny to hug me like this. There has never been a time that my dad hugged me. I wonder how it would feel to sit on Pretty Boy. I wondered if he would ride me like Jake. Did he ever think of me as his little girl? So many questions, and never an answer, for anything I couldn't understand. This is a lonely life for me.

Mama came home that weekend. I was so happy. It didn't take long before she pulled the old ironing cord from the wall. She beat me; I asked why. She said, "I am whipping your ass on, GP. You better shut up. I know your Granny don't whip you. I am just making up for lost time."

A few hours after the beating, she yelled, "Get in here, little Heifer. Go and get me a beer out the refrigerator." I was scared to tell her there was no beer in the refrigerator. Trembling, I said, "There is no beer here at all." She hopped up and beat me with the ironing cord again." My mama yelled, "You better not lie to me when I need a drink. Go search that refrigerator again." I ran in the kitchen. She followed and looked in the refrigerator. Mama said, "I guess my ole drunk daddy can't even leave a beer in the house. This is sad.

"Gal, you better get out there and go to the bootlegger. Get me a flat. Here is a dollar." I ran to Mr. Thomas and asked the lady for a flat. I told her my mama wanted it bad. The lady smiled as she took the dollar. She gave me the flat of clear liquid. I ran home to my mama. She snatched the liquor and said, "You are worth something . . . I don't know what. Now get out of my sight." I ran to the back porch and put a rag on the torn skin on my leg. I sat alone and cried myself to sleep.

Later on that evening, Granny woke me up. "Git up, girl, it time to feed the hogs before your great-granddaddy get home. He is off drinking somewhere." We carried the bucket of slop to the hog pen. The sirs had twenty-two little pigs. I named one of the pigs. My pig was a little brown baby pig with a white face. I played with my pig and told her how my leg was hurt from the beating my mama gave me.

I love talking to my pig. She would grunt and come close to the fence so I could rub her. I name my pig Coco. Grandma said, "Don't get too attached to that pig because one day she will be bacon, ham, neck, bones, and sausage." I didn't know what she was talking about. I was not going to let them hurt my pig. I told Coco all my secrets. She couldn't tell anybody, so I would talk to her a long time.

When we got back home, Poppy was lying on the floor drunk. We tripped over him. Grandmama said, "Just leave him where he is, at least he is here at home, with us. The last time he was very drunk, he went to his woman's house and stayed with her three days. I dared not say anything. He will beat me and maybe leave us. Then we would have nothing. That's life, gal, get used to it. We were born to take care of men." I felt so bad for my Granny.

She was scared of my granddaddy's shadow. I wonder if this was the way my life would be when I grow up. I heard a noise at the back door. It was our rescuer—Jake; Ok quietly, he came into the house. He shook his head and said, "Mrs. Mattie, why didn't you wait for me? You know I will always feed the hogs when Mule is drunk."

His words reminded me of the bad weekend before. Yeah, I remembered last Friday my great granddaddy was too drunk to walk and Jake had to feed the hogs. He took me with him. This day he picked up my little pig and brought her outside to play with me. Coco ran over to me. She rooting and grunted as she rubbed against my foot. Coco played with me a very long time. After a while, Jake had some corn in his hand and lured the baby pig back into the hog pen. "Let's go, big girl." We sang all the way home.

Today a week later, Poppy is very drunk again. He can't even crawl. He keeps falling back down every time he tried to get up. Jake picked my great-granddaddy up and put him in the bed. Softly, Jake whispered, "Don't worry, Ms. Mattie, Poppy will sleep all night and probably into Sunday afternoon.

"Tomorrow is Sunday, so he will be all right. The two of you can go to church without any trouble. Here is some money for church for you tomorrow." Grandmama smiled, saying, "No, Mule would kill me, and if he found out I took money from another man."

Jake

"Don't worry," he said, "your husband said he feels like I am his son. Well, your play son is giving you church money. Don't forget I am not like your son, Pretty Boy. You know how your son doesn't have time for anyone but his self. Your play son Bo is here all the time, whenever you need me."

Jake, Grandma, and I sat around the table in the kitchen that Saturday evening. The three of us ate supper together. Jake left after we finished eating. Grandma and I sang as we cleaned the kitchen. It was very hot in the house. When we finished cleaning in the kitchen, we went outside on the front porch to cool off. The mosquitoes were biting us everywhere. Grandma slapped and killed some of the biting bugs.

Out of the dark, Jake appeared, spraying away the bugs. "Don't worry, my ladies. Ole Bo can't stand the idea of something biting those precious legs and arms. These bugs are so bad they might try to bite you under your dress. I can't allow that to happen."

When the haze from the bug spray settled, Jake sat on the front steps. He said, "Mrs. Mattie, I brought you an extra something to help you get through all this craziness of Mule." She smiled and said, "Thank you, son, I need my tottie tonight. This has been a hard evening for me." We began to sing. It was fun. After a few songs Granny got quiet. She nodded off to sleep. Jake said, "Come here, Emma. You are getting to be a young woman." I smiled and said, "That's what my daddy said the last time he was home."

I sat down beside Jake. He said, "No, ma'am, your place is up here." The strong hands lifted me into my saddle. "Let's ride, little rider." I relaxed and enjoyed the ride. "You are safe with me. I promised your grandma I would take care of you." I laid my head back and enjoyed my horsey ride. He kept singing for a long time. We laughed and sang; he made me feel happy. I was smiling and eating my caramel sugar daddy candy. It was getting late. Grandma was snoring.

I said, "Okay, I am ready to go in the house." Jake snapped. "Oh no, not yet, big girl. Let's have a little more fun, okay?" We kept singing. I felt something punch me. "What is that?" It made me feel like I was sitting on that stick again. I yelled, "I don't like that stick, it upsets me. Stop, Jake, I don't like sitting on my horsey when that hard stick is in the saddle. Please take it out of the saddle."

"Okay, big baby, I will take care of that ole stick." He moved the stick. He said, "I got rid of that ole stick." I think he moved it; it did not hurt me anymore. He was smiling. Jake's strong hands sat me back in the saddle. "Don't be scared. This is what a big girl does."
"I don't like it."
Jake put his hand over my mouth and said, "Sh . . . sh . . . You will get used to this new kind of ride . . . Just let old Bo take care of you. Don't be so loud. Take it easy, big schoolgirl. Okay, just relax now and enjoy the last of your ride. Be quiet, sweet Emma, and let Granny finish her nap in peace. We have to take care of her."
My horsey kept rocking me. The saddle was no longer warm; it was very hot. This time it felt strange. I looked back as I felt wetness. My dress was wet in the back. I reached backward and felt the sogginess. What happened? The horsey has sweated on me. I hopped up and ran into the house.

I so am glad it was Saturday night. I filled the old tin tub. I soaked in the tub until I felt clean. I felt a burning between my legs. Riding in the saddle had irritated me. I rubbed the octagon soap on it and it smoothed the pain. I got out of the tub because I had to peepee. Oh, my god, it hurt so bad to pee. I yelled in pain. Granny was still sleep on the porch. She didn't even hear me scream. I got some of her Vaseline and salve and put it where it hurt. I hate that stick in the saddle. Why do I have to keep telling Jake I don't like that stick?

Tears washed my face. I wanted my mama. Can't somebody help me? I slipped back in the tub, shaking. I wanted to let the water smooth away my pain. Finally, I began to feel better. Later on, Grandma woke up and came in the house. She looked in the kitchen and saw I was safe in the tub. She said good night.

The next morning, I could still fell the soreness. It is going to take a while to get used to that saddle. I was scared to say anything to Granny. I feared that she and Poppy would fault me. Deep down inside, I thought they would get mad with me if I said anything about Jake. The two of them loved this man.

Bessie

Poppy woke up, took a bath, and dressed in his Sunday go meeting suit. Granny got up and cooked a full breakfast, as always. She smiled like nothing had happened on Friday night. She appeared content. It seem like she took the Friday night beatings as part of their regular life. We all got dressed. Granny straightened Poppy's bow tie. She said, "You look good, big boss man." He said, "Yes, gal, that's what happens when you have a nice wife like you." We walked to church. We got there before the morning service began. The three of us appeared to be very happy.

I love going to church. People were hugging and loving on one another. I felt so special in this place. Great-granddaddy Mule cut the grass around the church in the spring and summer. He boasts that he is part of the church staff. I call him Poppy; the adults call him Mule. Every Sunday he covers the money in the offering plate and puts it is the usher's room. He was a very important man in this church. No one ever said anything to my great-granddaddy about the way he treated his family when he was at church.

The usher always seated us on the opposite side of the church. We only saw Aunt Bessie in church. Bessie was the oldest child of my great-grandparents. She lived in another neighborhood. I didn't understand why Granny only daughter never came over to visit.

I asked Granny why Aunt Bessie doesn't come to the house. I wanted to play with her son. If he came over, I would at least have another child to spend time with. She had a handsome little boy.

That child never makes a sound in church. He seems to be a good boy. "How old is he, Granny?"

My dear Emma I don't know his exact age. She gave birth after she left my house. There is trouble in the midst of all of this. You are too young to be concerned about it. I gave birth to that child. My daughter Bessie was a good Christian girl. I raised her right. Bessie never talked back to me like your daddy. We enjoyed spending time together sewing. That girl is so talented. She made so many designer quilts that were displayed at the county fair.

Bessie was sewing so good that some of the ladies from the church hired her to make clothes for them. She was just ten years old then. My child had such a bright future."

"Mrs. Wade was Bessie's home economics teacher. She fell in love with Bessie. On the weekend, she would come and take my daughter home with her for the weekend. Mule did not like that, but he let her go with Mrs. Wade. When Bessie was in the fifth grade, Mrs. Wade came to me and said, 'Bessie is so smart we are going to have her tested to see if we can let her skip a grade.' I can't talk about it, baby. It hurts so badly. I miss my child Bessie I can't get involved."

This conflict was too painful for this ole woman. Granny shook her head and began to cry. "Your Poppy said our daughter Bessie can't come to his house anymore. He said she told a lie on him. Nobody believes those lies she told. Bessie got pregnant. She told the school teacher her daddy forced himself on her when he was drunk. The liar said he raped her over and over. I was sick in the hospital when it happened. When I came home, my child was gone.

"The court removed my daughter from our home. Mule told me he didn't want to hear that shit. That little wench got what she had been looking for . . . Mule claimed some little boy sneaked in to the house and had sex with that gal while he was at work. He said that little lying gal was trying to get him in trouble.

"The school social worker and counselor worked with the authorities to make Mule take a blood test. When they went to court Bessie was scared to testify against her daddy. She said Mule told her he would kill that little bastard if she testifies against him. The court protected Bessie. The test came back positive that he was the father. It is true the little boy you see with her is supposed to be Mule's child." Granny grunted, "I don't believe Bessie."

"It hurts me to have to choose my husband over my own child. She works and take good care of the little boy she name James. One day at church Bessie whispered in my ear and said, 'Mother, I name my boy after your father.' That broke my heart. I am glad she is back. She attended another church for a few years. It is so painful to see my child at church and know she has suffered all this by herself.

"It was so embarrassing when her foster mother came to church with her a few times. That lady rolled her eyes at Mule. We were introduced to each other. I thank her for what she has done for my child. When Mule saw me talking to the lady, he walked up and said, 'Listen up, my woman, it is time to get home and give me my Sunday dinner.

"He said, 'I think I want something sweet after dinner. Maybe you can give me some of your chocolate pie with white icing on the top.' That made me feels so shames. He winked his eye at Bessie. Then he walked between me and the lady. He said, 'You know what I mean Mattie. All of this chocolate pie is mine. Nobody else can have any of my pie baby. Ain't, that right Mrs. Mattie.' Bessie and I were so humiliated. He smiled and walked off. I saw tears in my daughter's eyes. That was so evil of Mule.

"Mule is a good provider. I can't visit my daughter Bessie and she can only see me at church. I love my daughter, but Mule is the head of our house." Tears washed her face. She wiped her face with her handkerchief. I started to cry. My poor granny has been through so much.

I understood the fear Granny felt. When my great-granddaddy was mad and drunk, he would chase us out of the house. He scares me so bad. My great-granddaddy is a big tall man. When he was drunk and mad, I and Grandma had to run away from home. We would run to Sam Hinton family's house and hide. The wife was a pistol-carrying woman, and everyone knew it. In fact her husband bragged about taking her hunting with him. No one would dare mess with this family. We would run there for safety. Quickly, they would put us in their closet.

A little while later, Poppy would figure where we were hiding. He would stagger down the road about three blocks from our house. Knocking on the door, he demanded me and Granny to come out. We hugged and trembled when he was beating on Mr. Hinton's front door. God only knows what he would have done to us if he could have got to Granny and me.

Most times Mr. Hinton the father was home. When he opened the door, you could hear the big bad wolf in my Poppy's voice back down. Mr. Hinton would always say, "You know better than coming up here to my house disrespecting my family. Go home now. We will get your family home later."

A few hours later, the wife and husband would take us home. First Mr. Hinton would go inside and make sure my great-granddaddy was asleep or sobering up. If he was still mad, Mr. Hinton would take us back home until later in the night. They saved us from many beating. Yes, it was a battle to stay out of the way of a big mad drunk man called Poppy.

One of the church members looked at me and said, "I don't know what Mule is mad about. There is something going on. He won't talk about it. I think his conscience is bothering him how he took advantage of that innocent child. He knows what he done was wrong. Everybody in this community knows he got away with it— most of all, God knows. His conscious is bothering him about taking advantage of poor Bessie. All of us in the community know that your granny is his punching bag."

Later, another lady from the church, Mrs. Hanes, said, "A drunken man's word is a sober man thought. We colored folk have a lot of pain and bad experiences. Most of us know God is our refuge. Faith in God is more than coming to church and hearing the word of God. That what I think is wrong with your great-granddaddy. He seems to have more faith in the whiskey bottle than he has in God."

Emma

The years flew by. I was eleven years old. I dream of going to Detroit where my mama lived. She always said no when I asked her to let me come and stay with her. Mama would say, "Little heifer, I don't have time to fool with you. You better stay here. At least you got somewhere you can eat and sleep because I can't give you that. Don't keep asking me the same question, because you will get the same answer no every time." Over and over she said no to me, it broke my heart. This has not been a good year of memories for me.

Now it is clearer to me at twelve years old my mama doesn't love me. She definitely doesn't want me around her. After the tears and hours of loneliness, I know I have my great-grandmother and great-granddaddy's love. Both has never told me they love me but they show it every day they feed and clothe me. I know this family gives me the best they can. I got a bed of my own. My great-grand-parent always made sure I go to school. They take care of me the best they know how.

Oh, I wonder if life would be better for me when I become a woman. The next morning I woke up in bed and there was blood on the sheets. I screamed. Granny came running in my room. "What's wrong, gal?"

"Look," I said. "There is blood in my bed, and I don't know how it got there. I don't remember hurting myself. How did this happen? Can you take me to the doctor?"

"No, my innocent child." Granny took my hand and said, "This is a part of growing into womanhood." She left and return with a box of Kotex. "This is yours now." She opened the box and gave me one. "Do you know what this is?"

I said, "No, Granny. The writing on the box says Kotex."

"Did they teach you about this in school?" Granny smiled and said, "No one taught me either when it happen to me as a girl. That day it happened to me, my mama gave me a pad made from some clean white sheets. It had cotton in the middle. We had to burn the pad after I used it. Today, we can go to the drugstore and buy Kotex. Oh lord, baby, your mama should be here to teach you about these things. Well, I will do the best I can. You come with me. You are going to get cleaned up and start wearing this Kotex."

I took a bath. We washed and rinsed my sheet in the big tin tub until they were sparkling clean.

This was a very scary time for me. I felt so alone. I got my rag doll and swung way up high. The swing carried me high, high in the sky—I felt so free. Life is different now. I don't know what womanhood is. Maybe one day Granny will tell me; until then, I will have fun with Ann my doll.

The summer is here. We have a lot of vegetables in the garden. Granny called me to the kitchen. "Come here. gal. I am going to teach you how to can fruits and vegetables. Listen, my precious little baby grand, we always can food when it is plentiful. When winter comes, we will always have enough food to feed our family. This is the way wise women takes care of their family. One day you will have a house of your own."

That summer we canned everything. We made big pots of soup. Grandma had quarts and pint jars. We canned every vegetable in the garden including the okra. Later we canned peaches, pears, figs, plums, and watermelon rinds. The jars of food look so pretty, high on the shelf in the kitchen. I was so proud of myself.

When we finished canning Grandma said, "You need clothes gal. She said come on we are going to the store and buy some clothes. I am going to teach you how to sew. If you do well, I will buy you better cloth at Brown Dollar Basement." I found some pretty floral cloth. We brought three yards of pink material and one yard of white for the trim. Grandma said, "Okay, I am going to show you how to cut a pattern out of newspaper. When I worked at the white folk's house, they gave me the newspapers. I used the paper to make patterns, wallpaper, and anything else I needed."

The next day, Grandma called me. The yellow measuring tape was wrapped around my waist. "Okay, you are twenty-four inches in the waist. Next we are going to measure your breast. Lord of mercy, you are going to have a chest like your mama. Your chest measures 38. That means you will wear a 38-size bra.

"I am so surprised at how your chest filled out so early. Most girls your age do not have a full chest like this, my sweet baby. Your young breast is big. We might have to buy you a 38C cup. No wonder your blouses fit so tight. Let's see how long the skirt should be, forty inches. You are tall for a young girl, so we will make your dress long. This will cover your knees well. A lady should keep her knees covered."

Grandma sat down on the floor with her scissors in her hand. "Come on, gal, we are going to cut a pattern just for you." She cut the material and began to sew my dress by hand. It was so pretty. I felt like a princess. On Sunday, I wore my new dress to church. Everyone was smiling. They said, "You are wearing such a pretty dress. Oh, little Emma, you are growing to be such a pretty big girl. Where did you get this pretty dress from?" I looked back and said, "My Granny made it for me." I had great pride in my handmade clothes. Some of the girls my age made fun of me at school. They said, "I wear store-brought clothes." I think I was supposed to feel shame, but I didn't. I felt good knowing how to make my own clothes.

Poppy

I was flying around the room like an eagle wearing my new outfit I made. I just had to wear it. I was modeling like the girl in the fashion show on television. An hour or so later, I was tired and hot and laid down to rest. I was exhausted. I slept a long time on the couch after modeling and prancing around the house. The material was thick and hot, it was a winter outfit. Lying on the couch, the fan blew cool air under my big pleated skirt. I slept a long time on the couch.

Poppy came home early on this afternoon. Granny was gone to missionary meeting at the church. I felt something under my skirt. I looked up; it was Poppy. He had his head under my clothes. He said, "All right, little gal, let me see what I got under here. This is my official duty as head of the power's house. It is necessary for the man with the authority over you to check his asset. This benefit is only for me. I am compelled to do my duty. No one else can complete this task.

"I am the only one that can make this determination, if you are average, regular, or great. It is my responsibility to declare your value. A man needs to know how much a heifer is worth. When Bessie was this age, I had to test her out and determine her value." I was puzzled. I said, "What are you doing to me, Poppy?"

He said, "Be quiet. Sh . . . sh . . . You got to just relax and cooperate with Poppy, and this won't take long. Legally, this is my time, just the two of us together. You are always with your granny. Time is running out, you are twelve years old now. I should have done this when you were eleven years old. I am behind on my schedule. All is well. Mattie has been watching this little jewel. I know she will keep guard over your virginity.

"You must understand the rules around this house. I am the man that will decide your fate. Mattie doesn't know what a man is willing to give for you. There are certain qualities that are very important to a man. It doesn't matter what any woman say.

"I know today is my magic Monday. Mattie leaves you alone only on Monday afternoon. This took careful planning. She can't be around when I do this kind of work. We got one good hour for this inspection. I plan to enjoy this hour of checking my stock. Your Poppy has been careful watching you." Poppy bragged, "I told the men that I ride with I had an early appointment, so I left in time to get here right after Mattie left. Matter of fact, I watched her leave out of the back door. I came in the front door.

"A man knows what another man wants. A man looks for more than just a good girl. He wants certain physical attractions that grasp his eye. The great thing is I see you have a rich treasure on your chest. These are great selling points. You were born with certain bonus that draws the attraction of a man's eye.

"I am your Poppy. This ole man has been watching you since you were eight years old. You draw my attention every time I see you. It is hard for me to restrain myself sometimes. This beautiful skin is as smooth as silk. I just want to touch these pretty legs. This is unreal for a girl your age to be so pretty. Emma, you are beautiful.

"Has anybody ever told you that?" I was so scared. Trembling, I said, "No, sir."

"Well, you belong to me. I have the rights to test what I see. Ole poppy loves what I feel here."

"Yes, sir, I am glad you are pleased with me, Poppy. Are you through now?"

"Hell no, I haven't got started yet. Shut up and be still." Sniffling, I pleaded, "Please don't beat me like you do Granny. I haven't done anything wrong, Poppy. I have been a good girl. Poppy I have done nothing but act like a young Godly girl just like they teach us in Sunday school."

"That's good girl."

I said, "Please don't hurt me like you do, Granny."

He smiled and said, "Don't worry, gal. Emma I need you to go in the corner of the living room and turn on the light." I rushed over to the corner. He yelled, "Surprise." Poppy had made a house out of sheets. It was a cute little house in the corner of the living room. It looked like a playhouse. I said, "Oh, what a pretty little house. Can I have my friend over to spend the night so we can play in my new house? It is so pretty. Where did you find the green and yellow sheets?"

He smiled. He said, "I bought them a few months ago and hid them from Mattie." Poppy smiled and said, I" built this house just for you. No, your friend cannot play in this house with you. This playhouse is private. I made is just for me and you.

Yeah, we are going to play hide and seek in this little house of yours. This is a new playtime for us." I went over closer and looked in the house. He pushed me inside the little house. When I looked around, he was gone A few minutes later he called out, "Emma, my little Emma, Poppy is looking for you. Where are you?" I was quiet. "Come out now, girl. Has anybody seen my Emma? Oh, I must find my little treasure." I was hiding in the corner of the little house. He kept calling; I did not answer. Then there was silence for a few minutes. He rushed in and yelled, "I found you!

"Where is my treasure, little girl?" I said, "I don't know, Poppy. I haven't seen it."

He said, "Oh yes you did. You are hiding it from me." Quickly he pushed me down. I fell backward. Now I was lying on the floor in the house he made out of sheets. "Be quiet, gal. I know you thought you got away. No such luck. I got you right where I want you now. You hid and now your Poppy is seeking. Let me see what you have hiding under this big thick skirt." I was so scared. I was trembling I said, "Please don't beat me like you beat Granny."

"Don't worry, little girl. Poppy got to do a different kind of beating in you. I am going to beat my ding dong in that hot oven of yours. I need you to be quiet and cooperate and it will soon be over." I said, "I don't want to play this game." He yelled, "Shut up and let me check you out.

"Be a good girl, little Emma. This dam big skirt is in my way." He pushed my skirt over my face. I started kicking him trying to get up. He lay down on top of me. His big body now covered me. I couldn't move. He grunted. "I am in charge, you can't go anywhere." Now Poppy is pressing me down on the floor. Crying, I yelled, "I have been a good girl, Poppy. Stop now! You are smothering me. I can hardly breathe with your big body covering me up. Please don't hurt me."

"I am glad you are a good girl. That makes your value shot up. Stop all of this kicking. I must evaluate my precious treasure. Let me get a better look at you. Let me touch that nice butt now. Poppy needs to check what's under this big heavy skirt. All this material is in my way I must get a better view of what I own. Poppy got to examine this stock right now."

I tried to get loose. His strong arm held me close to him. Poppy unbuttoned my skirt and pushed the waist of my skirt up over my bra. He squeezed my breast and rubbed my stomach. Then he put his hand into my panties. I tried to twist away from him. I yelled, "Stop, I don't want you to touch me like this, Poppy. You are a big man hurting a helpless child like me."

He snapped, "Shut up you can't tell me what I can touch." Now Poppy was rubbing my leg. His big hand went farther up my thigh. This frightened me. I asked, "What are you doing, Poppy?"

"I am checking Poppy's property." He snatched my bra loose. He said, "Oh yes, they are almost ready. My, my yours tits are bigger than Mattie's, and you are just twelve years old. They are nice and firm too. That is damn good. I got a treasure in these sweet babies.

"Oh yes, a man will pay a high premium for this. Your Poppy likes young tender meat. This rosy juicy meat is just what I have been looking for. Oh yes, I must keep a closer watch on you. Poppy must hurry and sample this meat before some man makes you his prize. It won't be long. Offers will start rolling in on this coochie. Have any those little boys at school touch you yet?"

I said, "Poppy, I have no interest in boys now. All I dream of doing is finishing high school. My goal is to go to college and become a teacher."

"You do that, sweet Emma. Stay focused on those books. I will keep my focus on my young coochie here." Poppy pushed his hand inside my panty again.

Poppy was grinning as he said, "I can't stop touching this sweet peach fuzz. This feels so good I can't wait to get inside. I like it? Oh yeah. Look, sweet Emma, what you have done." He took my hand and put it on the front of his pants. "Touch this, sweet baby girl. You just charge the ole man up. This is woman power with a girl's age. Baby Emma, you make Poppy feel so good. Yes, sir, I like this. You got this ole man hard and ready now. I can't wait any longer."

He pinned me down on the floor again. "I got to get inside of my new hot oven. Oh yes." He unzipped his pants and pulled his penis out, smiling. Holding me down, Poppy pointed his penis toward my panty. Fear came over me. I yelled, "Poppy what are you doing? What are you going to do with that?"

He laughed, "I must beat my meat."

"Is this what you are going to beat me with? What are you going to do to me? I promise I will be a good girl if you let me go."

"Yes, this is what Poppy is going to beat you with. It is useless begging me to stop. I have no control over getting hard. Once it fills up, I must empty it. This dick is harder than it has been in a long time." He reached over my skirt and waved his fat penis at me. He said, "Look at it, gal, see what you did to me. Now my sweet girl, your owner must get some relief. Your master must release himself. There is no way can I stop now. Nature has taken over. You don't understand, baby girl. Poppy can't control this. I must get inside this coochie now. This is the only way I can get any relief. I have not been this hard in many years. The only relief I can get is to get inside of you." He was very mad now. He said, "I am going to rip these drawers off they are in the way of your Poppy's progress. Matter of fact, you don't need these little draws on during my inspection." He reached down and snatched my panties off.

This big man started smiling. "Goodness gracious look at this precious hairy jewel of mine. It looks so good and pure. My goodness, gal, this is the prettiest treasure I ever inspected. This is better than Mattie's when she was a girl. Ole Mule has lucked up on a brown diamond." He sat back on my legs. His long arm reached inside my legs and pulled them open. Now this ole man played inside my vagina. Poppy was making funny noise like someone sucking on a lollypop. "Little Miss Emma, here I go. I got to stamp this as my own personal property. There is nothing in Poppy's way now. Nobody can stop this. I must put my personal brand on you. Be quiet and trust me. Lie down and stop fighting me. Yes, my sweet little peach, you do not have a choice. Stop kicking. I told you once, little gal, if you don't, I am going to slap you like I slap your Granny. I must get inside this hot coochie now. Once inside, I can check how tight and good it is. Then and only then can I put my dollar value on this. You can't get away from me. A man has strong power to take what he wants. I want to enter you to make my determination."

Holding me down, Poppy struggled to get his penis in me. I kept wiggling. He started smiling as he said, "Poppy got the head almost in. You are so tiny down here, yet you have a big body for your age." I fought while he struggled to keep me down. The telephone rang. Thank God the loud sound of the telephone scared Poppy. He didn't answer the first three rings. He kept trying to get inside of my body. This strong man kept rubbing my breast. He was fumbling as he yelled, "Who in the hell is that calling?" He said, "I better answer this phone, it might be Mattie calling to check on you from church." Finally he jumped up to answer the phone. I ran out doors with my bra hanging off. I grabbed my blouse. I was very scared as I ran with no panties on. I was trembling and hid under the back porch.

I heard him calling me. "Don't make me look for you, little heifer. Come on back in here so I can finish my inspection. This is a must requirement for the head of the Powers family. It has got to be done. You are wasting our precious time. Mattie will be back soon. Come here now. There is no way you can get around it. You can't get away from Ole Poppy. I demand that you git out here now. I am not going to let you get away from me.

"Ask Bessie, she will tell you Mule never stops until he gets what he wants. I must check the temperature in that young kitty of yours. That young hot kitty belongs to Ole Poppy now. I hope you know that. That's right, your tight young kitty belongs to me until you are married."

A few minutes later, Granny came home. She was shocked. "Did I hear you yelling at Emma? What did she do for you to yell at her like that? You sound like you were mad. Where is she? What did you need her for?" Poppy grunted. Granny said, "It is just four o'clock. What happened? You are home early."

He said, "I had to come home and check on the stock. You need to know the value of what you own. It is a must for ole Mule to be aware of his valuables. I must check out all of our assets. I got to evaluate things around here every now and then. I wrote down the value of the pair of goats, three boars, six sirs and twenty-two pigs I own. So, Mrs. Mattie, I am taking inventory of everything of value on this place. This is a man thing. Stay in your place and all will be well. This is my obligation to be responsible for whatever I possess. Stay out of my business and you will be all right.

"How was Bible study, Mattie?"

Granny said, "It was very good. We cut it short because some of our members are getting older they had to go home before it gets dark. Many are sick and shut in. Where is Emma?"

Poppy said, "I don't know. I am not her keeper. She is some-where around here." I went down near the hog pen and cried. I heard Granny calling me. Finally, I went home.

She said, "You had me worry. Are you okay?"

I said, "Yes, ma'am. I was so happy about my new outfit I went to show Coco my new clothes. I am so happy, I cried."

Granny said, "It is good that you take pride in what you have made. Come on now let make supper." She asked, "Mule have you fed the hogs yet?"

He yelled, "Not yet. Where is that little gal?" I didn't answer. He yelled, "Come on, Emma, you got to help me with the hogs. Your Granny can handle the kitchen. I want to see your little baby pig." I came into the room.

I said, "Granny, I thought you were going to teach me how to make an apple pie?" Granny smiled and said, "Your Poppy needs you to go with him. He is the boss. Whatever Mule tells us to do, we must follow his orders. Always remember, Mule controls our lives. He is in charge of this place. Go on now, don't make him mad because we all will be in trouble. Just do whatever he wants you to do. That is simple. He knows what is best for us. Never forget he is in charge of everything around here. We can cook the pie on another day."

I walked slowly behind Poppy to the hog pen. When we got to the hog pens, I was so scared. His voice had changed. He sounds like a big bad wolf. His thick beard started at one ear and made a half circle on his face. His big beard was gray and white. It looked like Santa Claus's. He told me to come and get the corn from the bucket he was holding. When I reached into the bucket, he gripped my hand. Quickly, Poppy led me over near the shed. He rubbed my breast. He began to grunt. He said, "My, my how I need to get up in my young hot coochie right now."

Poppy sat on an old bucket. He said, "Come here, gal." I was scared. I said, "Poppy can we wait and do the inspection later? I don't want Granny to be mad if we are late." He unzipped his pants. Poppy sat me on his lap. Quickly he tried to stick his penis in me again. He said, "Oh yes, I am going to take me a quick piece before we go back to the house." I was trembling. He was moving his body as he pushed against my vagina. "Hmm, this is going to be good." Granny yelled out, "Emma what is taking y'all so long? Is something wrong down there?"

He yelled, "Hell no, stay your ass up there and fix my supper."

"Mule, can you hear me. Do you need me to come down and help with the livestock?"

Poppy got very mad. He said, "I don't want to whip Mattie's ass this evening. She would have a heart attack if she saw me inspecting this coochie. I need this now."

Granny yelled, "I am on my way down there. If it's taking you this much time, you need help."

He yelled, "Stay up there if you know what is good for you. I am on my way, woman." He stood up and zipped his pants. He was so mad he said, "If Mattie wasn't home, I would take you in this ole shed. That ole woman of mine loves you so much she will come down here. If you are gone too long, she will come looking for you. She should be glad I found another hole to stick this dingdong in. You better not tell anybody about me checking out our merchandise. Just remember, I was interrupted, but I must finish what I started. You belong to me just like these pigs and my sires. I will put you out of my house just like I did Bessie if you ever mention it to anybody. Then where will you go? We are the only family that wants you, little girl. Inspecting you are my rights and mine alone."

I was trembling. I said, "Poppy I won't tell anybody that you checked me out to see about your valuables. Is that right?"

"Yes, that is right big gal, you are prime meat." He snapped, "Never forget that as long as you are under my roof, I am in charge." I was crying. I said, "Poppy I know you have power over us. No one can make me tell about being inspected by you. You are in charge." Poppy smiled, saying, "You got that right. Trust me, I am going to finish my inspection as soon as possible."

This was the most frightening time of my life. All I wanted to do was forget this day. We ate supper. I was so scared. I told Granny I wanted to read in my room. I lost myself in books. I read every day trying to forget the fear I feel when I see Poppy. I made sure to stay out of his way. Believe me, I don't want to lose my home like Aunt

Bessie. Now I feel so alone. I can't tell Granny. Now Jake is my only protector. It is too embarrassing to even tell Mr. Jake Brown.

This week was long and scary. Every day I would hide when Poppy came home from work. I have a basket of books to read. The lady at the library said they were going to discard the books. I said, "Please give them to me." She did. I told Granny I was going to take a week and read as many books as possible. She smiled and said, "You were born to be a teacher. I think you love books more than anyone I know." I said, "Thanks, Granny. That's quite a compliment." She said, "You seem to like using all those fancy words you are learning." I said, "Yes, Granny these books give me power."

Wednesday afternoon, Granny said, "Come, my child, we are going to revival." We rode the bus across town. The church was full of people by the time we arrived. The choir from our church Faith Missionary Baptist sang all the songs that night. Our pastor preached. His subject was "Train up a child in the Way they should go." This subject made me sad. Did this mean Poppy was training me up the right way? He told the young people it is written that a child should obey your parents. I said under my breath; I am not going to obey Poppy if he tries to inspect me again.

I love the part where the pastor encourages us to study. I study hard and obey my teachers. Reverend said, "Children, you should respect authority, and you will succeed." In my heart I said it is hard for me to respect Poppy's authority. This was confusing for me. Any way I learned some new scriptures. We attended all three nights of revival. It was nice to get out of our neighborhood.

Granny seemed the happiest when she was away from home. She acted like a different person. I noticed she would linger and talk to folk in the church as long as they would listen. Sometimes Granny would just stand and listen to the ladies. The lonesome look in her eyes would disappear when she was away from Poppy.

Sometimes she would walk over to Mrs. Liza's house. This is an old lady that lived alone. She was ninety-five years old. She said, "My children all are gone. I am losing my sight." Mrs. Liza said, "Thank you sister, Mattie, for remembering me and bringing me some of your canned food. This is such a blessing. Do you have time to read to me?" Granny said, "Yes, I do. I have a surprise for you. I am going to let Emma read to you. She is so smart in school." I read ten chapters of Proverbs to Mrs. Liza. She began to cry. "It is so nice to hear the word of God. I can't see how to read anymore. Granny, and I cleaned Mrs. Liza house before we left. Granny and I sang all the way home. We were so happy.

Sunday morning we got dressed and went to church together. Granny was dressed up in a pretty blue flower dress. She wore a white hat with a blue ribbon around the brim. Oh my goodness, she looked so pretty. Poppy wore a blue pinstripe suit, with a white shirt and blue bow tie. He looked like a gentleman that loved his family. I wore my new blue-and-yellow dress. Many ladies gave us compliments. We looked so nice and normal.

When morning services was over, the pastor and his wife stood outside and talked. Soon everyone was gone. Poppy said, "I am too tired to clean the church this evening, Pastor. I always do my part to help out. This church is known throughout town as a community church taking care of the less fortune ones around us."

Bessie

On this special Sunday afternoon, Granny let me stay for junior mission. We had a great time. This group of girls was being trained to become missionaries. On this day we made special gifts. Making pretty baskets were fun. We made sure each basket was packed with a book of scriptures, lotion, creams, a bright fresh fruit, and canned food the ladies made at home. There were big juicy colored red apple in the center to make the basket pretty. Each basket was wrapped with clear paper. The bright bow made it special and cute. We made twenty thanksgiving baskets for the elderly. Bessie was one of the advisors. Aunt Bessie said we would deliver the baskets on Wednesday, the day before Thanksgiving. She said, "I wish we could spend more time together, Emma." I said, "I do too."

When everyone left it was just the two of us in the fellowship hall. She walked over to me and asked, "How do you like living with my parents?" Proudly, I said, "Life with my Granny is great. She is very good to me. I couldn't ask for a better woman to love and be there for me. She makes sure I get what I need. It makes me sad to see how Poppy treats her." Aunt Bessie walked up to me and hugged me. She said, "Be careful around my daddy. Try not to be alone with him." I dropped my head trembling. She said, "Oh no, has he touched you?" I began to cry.

We stood even closer together. Aunt Bessie said, "Let me tell you what happened to me. I am sure no one else can or will. My mother got very sick. Deacon Austin let my father drive Mother to the doctor. She was too sick to ride the bus. The doctor sent her to the hospital to be admitted.

This was a scary time. My daddy and I stayed with her over twelve hours in her hospital room. Everyone was concerned about my mama. Some of the ladies from the church rushed out to the hospital to see about her. Tears were rolling down her face as she continued. Mule cried and patted my mother's face in front of the members from the community and church. A couple of the men embraced him and said, 'We are praying for you and your wife.' Poppy was so sad. He said, 'I can't stand leaving my wife here, but somebody has to take care of my Mattie's baby girl Bessie. My wife has been hurting for a long time. It is time she gets some help. I know she needs this medical treatment. We have never been away from each other since we married thirty years ago. It is going to be hard on me without my Mattie at home with me.' My mother cried with him. She told him she should be better in a few of days.

"The three of us was very sad at the hospital. We left the hospital. Poppy drove the car home and didn't say a word to me all the way home. The car belonged to one of the deacons. The deacon told Poppy he could use the car to get back and forth to the hospital. The old deacon had gotten too old to drive his car. Poppy drove Deacon Austin around sometimes. I felt sad for Poppy.

"He drove home and fed the livestock. Later that evening, our next-door neighbor came over. She brought dinner for Poppy and me. Mrs. Ella asked Poppy, 'Why you don't let young Bessie stay with my daughter Bernice until Mattie gets home? I can do her hair and take care of her.' Poppy thanked her and said, 'Mattie has trained this little gal very well, if we run into problems, I will let you know. Thank you for the meal. Mattie got food canned up here. We have enough food to last a year. You know how Mattie is. She always looks out for her family.' Mrs. Ella got up from the chair. She gave me a big hug. She said, 'If you need anything, just let me know, Bessie.' I smiled and said, 'Okay.' Mrs. Ella walked down the steps. She looked sad as she left me.

"This woman has seen and heard my Poppy beating my mother many times. Many times after the beatings, she would come over when Poppy leaves home mad. He said so many nasty, degrading comments when he gets paid. He makes sure we know he is supporting us. My mother said we just have to learn to live with it. Mrs. Ella turned around and said, 'Bessie, you let me know if anybody hurt you, okay?' I said, 'Yes, ma'am.'

"Poppy changed when Mrs. Ella left. Poppy grunted and slammed the front door. He put on a good show at the hospital in front of the church members . . . He turned on the television. Smiling, he said, "We need some happy sounds up in here. Ella needs to take care of her own home and leave mine alone." This television's noise made the house seem alive. I felt safe. Mother always said Poppy loved me and he would always take good care of me if something happen to her.

"After Mrs. Emma left, I was miserable. I went to my room and cried myself to sleep. Then it was just the two of us in the house. The smallest bedroom was mine."

I sighed, "You mean the room I sleep in now?"

She nodded yes. "Emma, your room was once my room."

Aunt Bessie said, "My daddy waited until my mother was sick in the hospital to take advantage of me. The house felt lonesome because my mother was lying up in the hospital. I was terrified. I missed her presence. The mere ideas that I could lose her rocked my world." Aunt Bessie sniffled as she continued to talk. She said, "I was asleep. The ole cuckoo clock struck 1:00 a.m. A few minutes later, my room seemed so peaceful and still. Something touched me. I jumped. I felt something pulling on my pajamas. I yelled, 'What is in here? Who is this?' He said, 'Who do you think this is? It is your boss, Ole Mule. You are eleven years old now, gal. Where I came from, when a gal gets your age, she is ready for service. This morning you will start servicing me in Mattie's place. You are already running this house like a woman. You swept the yard just like Mattie does. That is just part of the job running my house. Ms. Bessie, you are doing a fine job while your mother is sick. It is your responsibility to take her place in everything. Now while she is sick and unable to do her wifely duties, you will fill in for my old lady. You have done everything else. Mattie can't be here, and I need to ride a little bit. Hell, you don't have a choice. Little Ms. Bessie, you are required to supply for her.'

"I said, 'Poppy, what are you talking about. Supply what, Poppy?' He said, 'I will show you.' I was so confused. 'Where are you going to go riding this time of night? The car is locked outside. There is nothing in here to ride.' He yelled, 'Yes the hell it is. You are a hot little filly that I must ride tonight. I am going to check this merchandise out tonight. You know you belong to me, just like Mattie. I said, 'Yes, sir, Poppy, you are making me scared.'

"He picked me up and took me to the living room. He had a pallet made in the dark corner of the room, it was frightening. 'Here, little gal, I got something to calm you down.' I was crying. The cup of bitter stuff was horrible. I said, 'I don't want this.' He slapped me in the face. 'Shut up, little hot heifer.' I said, 'Please I don't like the way this tastes.'

"He yelled, 'Shut up, this is corn liquor.' I asked, 'Why do I need this?' He said, 'This will make it easy for both of us.' He pushed the bottle in my mouth and turned it up. He forced me to drink it. The liquor ran all over my chest. This bitter drink was so strong. Soon the room was spinning. I lay there. I tried to get up but couldn't. My own daddy stripped my pajamas off of me. This shocked me that the man I respected and trusted was kissing me all over. I could feel his big hand rubbing my breasts. 'You are a pretty little tender, young gal.' He whispered, 'Miss Bessie, grown folk call me Mule because I am big man with a long dingdong. I am very strong. I am going to do to you what a mule does with a young filly. Mule is going to ride this right now. You are prime little filly that has never been touched. Bessie, this is so fine'. His big leg forced my legs open. Now he put his hand in my vagina. I yelled, 'Daddy, what is wrong with you? What are you doing? Why are you doing this to me?' I was pleading, 'Daddy, I don't want to be out here. I want to go back to my room.' Mule grunted, 'No you are not going anywhere.' Quickly he grabbed me by my neck and pinned me down on the pallet. His body was so heavy. He shoved something hard into the hairs on my vagina. Poppy said, 'You got some thick hair around the hot hole.' I was so dizzy. He confused me. I didn't understand why he was talking so loud to me. I am sure Mule intended for the neighbors to hear him. Mrs. Ella's husband came home from work about one o'clock every morning. This first episode happened a few minutes after one o'clock. Mule's voice got louder. You know how close those houses are."

I said, "Yes, Auntie, I know. I am so sorry, Aunt Bessie."

She said, "Wait, let me go on. Poppy's hand started playing inside my vagina. He yelled, 'Relax, gal, I am going to make you feel so good. It is useless for you to holler. There is nobody that can help you. Your savior Mattie is old and sick in the hospital. I am in charge of this house. Yes, Bessie, this is my good-luck night. Mule is going to make a little woman out of you this morning. Relax, young gal.' He kept massaging my clitoris. 'Come on now, little heifer I am going to take it easy.' His hand went back to my breasts as he started pushing his hard penis inside of me. It wounded my inside so bad I was dizzy, but I yelled, 'Why are you hurting me like this?'

"Now I was mad. I yelled, 'Mule you are destroying my body. This is not right. A daddy should not do this to his daughter. Stop right now!' He grinned. 'There is no way, my young tender Bessie. You must supply my need right now.'

"Mule said, 'I need you to remember this day. I am making this your official duty.' This man started roughly forcing his way inside of my body. He paused and looked down at me. 'Good golly, Miss Molly, you sure feel good to me. Bessie, this sure is good stuff.' He yelled, 'As the head of the house, I must determine your value, sweet Bessie. I think this is premium stuff between these legs.' He rocked and twisted for a long time. The pain was as hard as giving birth to a child. Believe me, I know both. Mule didn't stop until he was inside of me. Finally, this sick old man was smiling. It seemed like a bad dream. My own blood daddy rode me until he got hot. He was sweating and began to yell. 'I want everybody to know I got a young hot coochie up in here. I have not had this much heat in this house for years.'

"This scared me. I thought something was wrong with him. I said, 'Poppy, what is wrong, are you sick? Are you getting too hot? Why are you hollering?' He looked down and said, 'Yes, ole Mule is on fire. You just scorched my dingdong with your sizzling coochie, Miss Hot Bessie. You did it to me, little gal. You make me feel like a king.' I felt a warm gush of something inside my vagina.

"This was the first time a man had ever touched me. Mule humiliated me on that pallet as he rode me. His body began to jerk as he plunged deeper inside of me. He yelled even louder, 'I want everybody to know I am up inside my new coochie this morning.' Mule sprayed warm thick mess inside of me again and again. His thick juice made me feel so nasty and dirty. I was forced to lie in his wet sticky juice.

"The clock stuck 3:00 a.m. Mule yelled, 'Thank you, sweet baby, for this hot coochie. This is a perfect present. Ho, ho, I am ole Santa Clause at sunrise. I just took the best gift a man can enjoy.' He was bragging this is a good ride. 'Can't nobody keep me out of this now. It belongs to Ole Mule now.' I was pleading, 'Sh . . . Sh . . . man. What is wrong with you? These neighbors will think I am a bad girl. We are in Mother's house and you are taking advantage of me. How can this be right? It was yesterday you were putting on that big show at the hospital talking about you couldn't go on without Mother. Now look at what you are doing now? This is not right my mother is in the hospital, and you are enjoying raping me. People in this community will end up calling me a whore.' Pleading, I begged, 'Quiet down now for my sake. Mrs. Ella is going to hear you.'

"Mule got off me and pulled me up between his legs. 'Baby, you are mine. I need them to know. I purposely raised my windows up and the curtains open. This was a sure way they can hear us. I am letting Ella and the rest of the nosey folk know what is what in my house. Ella has heard us with her own ears, and she can't do a damn thing about it.' It seemed like this went on forever. My world was turned upside down. There were no words to express how degrading this was to me.

"My head was spinning, thinking *What will the neighbors think of me now as they heard my daddy yelling my name calling my vagina a coochie?* When I woke up later that morning I was in my bed naked with mother's robe over me. How humiliating was that to cover his dishonored daughter with her mother's robe?

"I didn't want to get up. The phone rang. Mrs. Ella called to check on me. She said, 'Are you all right, Bessie? I thought I heard someone screaming over there this morning? Was that you? I wanted to call the police, but my husband told me to stay out of Mule's business.' I said, 'No. It was not me.' She paused.

"Mrs. Ella sniffled and said, 'Lord, help you child. I pray you will be all right over there with Mule. I know how he has treated sweet Mattie over the years. Nobody has to tell me anything. I hear and see. Anyway, baby, you can let me know if Mule beat you. Are you sure you are okay over there with Mule?' I assured Mrs. Ella everything was okay. I was trembling when I hung up the telephone.

"This telephone call made me nervous. It hurt me to walk, but I had to go to school half day to keep Mrs. Ella out of the house asking questions. Mule warned me before he raped me he would kill me if I said anything to anybody. I believed him. I have felt his rage many times before, as he berated me and Granny when he was drunk.

"Today is Tuesday, a school day. I went to school. It seemed like a dream. After school, I went to the hospital. Mama asked, 'Is everything all right? I said, 'Yes, Mama. She said, 'I am sorry, I have to stay in this hospital for a few more days. You look so sad. Have you been crying?' I said, 'Yes, Mother, I miss you.' She said, 'I am worried about you, baby. When I see you have been crying, it makes me sad. Baby, if it was left up to me I would ask Ella to keep you at her house until I got home. When I mentioned it to Mule, he pitched a fit. He said, "Hell, no. Bessie can't stay with Ella until you come home. Her place is at home with me. She needs to be at home helping out around the house. You have taught her well. Give Bessie a chance to prove how well she has learned from you.'" Mother said, 'Bessie you can use the vegetable soup in the fruit jars on the shelf in the kitchen.' Crying, she said, 'Mama will be home as soon as I can.' The week went on. My mother was in the hospital for ten more days.

"The first evening, Mule came back from the hog pen, and he told me to stand up. I was studying my homework. I was behind in my classes. I still had on my school clothes. He said, 'You are pretty little schoolgal. Come here to your teacher. I said, 'Why, Poppy?' He said, 'Do not ask so many questions.' I walked over to him. He was smiling. Poppy laid me across his lap and spanked me. He said, 'You have been a bad girl haven't you, little hot heifer? I am going to have to discipline you—no, I mean I am must dick you.' Mule pulled my panty off He flipped me over and pulled my blouse open. Poppy sucked my breast so hard. I was crying. I asked, 'What are you going to do to me now?' 'I am going to ride this little hot filly right now,' Mule said. 'I enjoy having control of this coochie.'"

My aunt was holding me so close, trembling and crying. She went on to say, "Emma, my daddy finished tearing into me the second night. The corn liquor he forced me to drink did not kill the pain as he rode me like a train. Nothing mattered to him. I was screaming and beating him on the face and head. It did not slow Poppy down as he forced his penis in me again. It felt like my female organs were jagged and bruised. He looked down on me and said, 'That's right, let the neighborhood know I can get schoolhouse pussy. Your home teacher is spanking your butt. You have been a naughty young gal.' Pleading, I said, 'Mule please take it easy on me today.' 'All right, Bessie, just because you are trying to be a smart ass, I am going bust this ass open.' He grabbed a pillow and carried me to the bathroom. He stuck the pillow in the sink and bent me over the sink. He began to laugh. He said, 'I bet this will make you holler.' This pain was a stabbing and tearing pain as he forced his penis in my butt. Mule yelled, 'Hell I am proud to let them know whose stuff this is. It is mine, all mine. They need to know I am not an old worn-out stud. I am still a good man in the bed.' I said, 'That's enough, isn't it, Mule? You have rammed this big long thing too far in me as it is. Stop now, I am tired and sore.' He reached around and slapped my face. He stared riding me again. Mule slapped my butt so hard I jumped. He yelled, 'Shut up all that noise. You are messing up my ride.' He did not stop pumping inside my butt.

"Emma, I can never forget those sounds he made as he pressed me down. My own daddy sounded like a big freight train pounding against the railroad tracks. He was bouncing from side to side. His heavy body began to splash in his sweat. In my heart, I knew Mrs. Ella and her family heard him yelling my name again today. Mule was yelling, 'This is a good fuck I got right here. Nobody can stop me from getting this coochie.'

"Mule laughed. 'Ella must be crazy. I am not going to let you spend the night over there. Hell, she got a husband and a son. They have been looking at you for a while. Her ole man said to me, "Mule, you better watch that little gal. She is fine as wine. I wouldn't mind getting that if I was just a little younger." I knew then I would have to kill him if he tried to get up in you.' Finally, Mule stopped for a while and went into the kitchen. He sat down and listened to the radio for a while. I struggled back into the room. I was so glad. I thought he had finish with me. I lay down on my bed. He yelled, 'Where is my supply heifer while Mattie is laid up resting? Come on now, gal, do not make me come in there and get you.' Mule yelled, 'Bessie, come quickly while my red rooster pill is working.'

"Listen, Emma, my daddy called me into the kitchen that night. I was so embarrassed. I found mother's robe and went to see what he wanted. Our kitchen window was up again. He had opened the curtains. I noticed the window was up in Mrs. Ella's kitchen. I was ashamed and scared. I said, 'Daddy they can see you.' 'That is right, I want them to see me fucking you. This is the way I can show them my authority.' He was sitting in the kitchen chair naked. 'Come closer to Ole Mule, sweet Bessie.' I asked, 'What do you want, Mule? I don't want people watching you take my body.' The man's long arm reached over and grabbed me. I pleaded, 'Can we go in the bedroom?' I said, 'Please don't disgrace me like that.' He sat me down on his lap and started to play inside my vagina. He pulled the robe off I was wearing. Now, I had no clothes. He smacked as loud as he sucked each breast very hard. He went down between my legs and played and thrilled my vagina. Mule started to brag; he said it has not been a week and this coochie is responding to its owner. Smiling, Mule said, 'See, Miss Bessie, I know how to thrill this coochie.' Quickly, he said, 'Now, it time for the show to start'. My daddy lifted me up and forced me down on his big hard penis. I screamed, 'Oh, Lord, please help me.' Mule said, 'Nobody can help you now.' I started to beg, 'I can't stand this. It feels like you are tearing my vagina to pieces, man.' He yelled, 'That's right, let the nosy folk know that I got my big fat hard dingdong rammed up in you knocking boot.'

"I was crying, 'Why are you forcing this big long penis inside me? I don't want you to do this to me. This is like a bad nightmare, it is so horrible. Please, Daddy, if you love me, you will stop.' He smiled and said, 'I do love you, and that is why I can't stop.' He started pumping upward into me harder and harder with each thrush. Mule was grinning. He pumped hot lava up inside of me. After a while, he stopped and rested. I tried to get down. He said, 'Not yet, this round is not over.' He eased me down on his penis again. I hate saying the word *penis*. It reminds me of that ghastly week. Listen, Emma, Mule stopped for a few minutes. I was moaning. He pushed me to my knees. Mule pulled my face up to his crotch. He tried to force his big penis in my mouth. It felt like two big hard cucumbers choking me, I couldn't breathe. I passed out. Later I came around and was still struggling to breathe. He said, 'Well, baby, your little mouth is too little for this dingdong. I am going to let you take a breather for the rest of the afternoon.'

"The next day I struggled to school, I could not focus on what the teachers were saying. The stinging in my body was too much, I left school early. When I got home, I went to bed and slept until dark. I heard him calling me. He asked, 'What is wrong? You were asleep when I got home.' I said, 'I feel nauseated.' 'Well, don't worry, this will help you.' Mule reached over and got the liquor. He made me drink some more corn liquor. He said, 'This is for the pain, baby. I know you might have a little tenderness and a wound or so that goes with your new job as a supply woman, baby, baby, but my new coochie makes me feels so good. Ole Mule was smiling at work. Every time I thought about it, I got a hard on. Ole Mule can't stop. I can't help myself.' He raped me over and over. He started about 1:00 a.m. again. I don't know what time he stopped. That was not the end. He continued to push against me until his balls were hitting my butt. Emma, do you know what that means?" I said, "No, Aunt Bessie." "My daddy's penis is almost as large as his arm. It looks like a horse's penis." She said, "That meant Poppy has forced his entire fat penis up to the balls inside of my tender body. I went numb. I was glad I was drunk for the rest of that torture. I don't know what else he did. Later, he took me to the bed and dropped me like a rag. There was no more strength in my body. I woke up the next day about twelve o'clock. I was too ashamed to go outside. My body was too weak. This was too much of a disgrace to go to church. I know I could not face Mrs. Ella.

"That Sunday afternoon, he came home smiling. He said, 'The ladies at church asked where you were, I told them you were having a little female problem this morning. Ha-ha, my sweet baby, what they don't know is that my Bessie had too much of Mule last night. Mule smiled and said I was bouncing around like a young cat at church today. It gave Ole Mule great pride taking possession of this coochie. I feel like a young buck. One of the ladies said, "Mule you look like you are feeling better." I dropped my head and faked being sad. I said I am getting better with Mattie being away from me. Oh, don't look so embarrassed. Don't you worry I told them I would have you at church for sure next Sunday. I know from experience you will be all right in about ten days. It is going to take me that long to polish my jewel in my young hot Bessie with the good coochie. That tight coochie will be adjusted to ole Mule's long fat tool by next Sunday, little woman. Those old women don't have a clue to what I have been up too—I mean I have been up in. Every inch of that jewel belongs to me. It is all mines now. I am a happy man this Sunday. This is a miracle. Mattie got sick at the right time. My sweet Bessie, you are the best supply gal a man could have wish for. Listen, little gal, you are getting the same treatment I gave your mother. Only thing different is I was younger and could ride much longer. Yes, Old Mule sent Mattie to the doctor several times when she was young. I first punched that coochie when she was ten years old. Yeah, I started pumping her at an early age. Those doctor visits went on for a few years until her body got used to her master's sweet rod.'"

Aunt Bessie and I sat down in the dining hall. It was very quiet. Aunt Bessie sobbed for a long time. I just held her close. Finally, she said, "Emma, my daddy is a big man. He will force himself on you like he did me. Believe me, baby girl, I can't tell anyone else in this world what I have told you. I don't want that to happen to you. It is a nightmare you can't wake up from. It will stay with you always. I will pray for you, Emma. I love you. Listen, Emma, that is not all he did to me. The third day, Mule came home early. He, said, 'The machine broke down at work. Ole boss said we could stay around and clean the yard. I told him, "No, sir, I am going home and check on my family. My wife is sick." He smiled and said, "Go ahead, Mule. Take care of your family. Make sure you supply all of their needs. If you need my help, let me know." Mule said, "I am supplying everything they need." 'I left the job with a smile on my face and a hard dick for my Bessie. I knew she was ready and waiting to satisfy my needs. When I got home from school, he was home very early. 'Well, little gal, I have fed the livestock. It is time for you to feed me.' On that afternoon, my daddy sat on the front porch and waved at the neighbors. One by one they asked how everything is going with Mattie. He smiled and said, 'Everything is going just fine. My dear Mattie is in good hands. They will take good care of her. Mattie just needs some much needed rest.'

"The worse memory is he waved at Mrs. Ella. She walked up to the porch. 'Mule, do you need me to do anything for Bessie or you?' 'No, thank you, Sister Ella, everything over here is great. I could not ask for a better gal to take care of stuff around here. Yes, young Bessie is a sweet girl supplying all of my needs.' I felt so shamed. Really, I felt worse than a whore. This ole goat sounded like he was bragging about his deeds. Yes, niece here was my daddy, sitting on our front porch, letting the neighbors know he was using me to supply his perverted sexual fantasies. He stared yawning. 'Well, Sister Ella,' he said, 'We had a long day, I think we will turn in early. See you later.' This was about five o'clock in the evening. Now there was nothing I could say to make Mrs. Ella think all was well. My life became a life of shame and humiliation. Mule got up and came inside, talking loud. He took off all his clothes and walked past the window.

"Emma, my daddy proudly showed his power over me as he strolled around in the house undressed. Now my daddy was inside the house yelling his sexual demands to me. He yelled, 'Come on, Bessie, get on your mama's side of my bed. You know you must perform her wifely duties till she gets back.' This made me scared. Mule said, 'We are going to turn in early, young gal.' Softly I whispered, 'Okay, Daddy. You can go to bed early I want to watch television.' He walked into the living room and stood in front of the television. 'No, Miss Bessie, there will not be any television for you tonight. I am the star in your show, sweet baby.'

"He walked back into the kitchen. I was shaking. He said, 'You have a choice: I want my coochie while the sun is shining. You can lie there and let me ride my pussy or die.' I thought he was going to kill me. Poppy shouted, 'Hurry up and drink that Kool-Aid I made. Getting off early has given me extra time. Now we have a longer time to enjoy our precious time together. Ole Mule added a little more corn liquor in your Kool-Aid to make it taste better for you. This shiny will help my innocent Bessie enjoy what ole Mule is going to give you.' I said, 'No, sir, I don't like the taste.' He walked around the table. He pulled me up and put the Kool-Aid in my hand. He said, 'Drink it or I will whip your ass. Stop wasting my time. Listen, gal, I was so horny for you. Ole Mule couldn't even go see my wife, Mattie. If she saw me this hard, she would faint. No, Bessie, I left my job early just for you. I need this coochie more than I need the money.' He was getting very angry with me. I sniffled and drank the Kool-Aid.

"He said, 'Finish it all, little hot heifer. This Kool-Aid is stronger than ever.' Poppy said, 'I didn't have time to go get anything else. This will do.' I went to the couch and sat down. I asked Mule, 'Why do I need to drink something, I don't like this corn liquor, it makes me drunk.' He jumped up and said, 'Because I said so, little bitch.' Mule scared me so bad that I became petrified. He said, 'It will relax you, my chili pepper. You excite me. Bessie, you got this dingdong hard, and it is still hungry for that hot pussy.' I was so confused. He was more focused on raping me than taking care of his wife. It was that very minute I realized that I hated this man. I could never call him my father again. Even until this day, I despised him for raping and molesting me repeatedly and getting away with it.

"The next day, I cooked breakfast before school. I came home and cooked dinner that evening. After he fed the hogs on the fifth day, his demand was worse. On this fifth afternoon, about 4:00 p.m., it started to rain. He grabbed me and said, 'You know what they say about rain.' I said, 'No, sir.' He said, 'Rain is family time. The rain falls on the roof and this let the man rain inside his girl or woman. That is when men make babies more babies than ever. I am not trying to make a baby, but I am going to enjoy our family time.' Mule yelled, 'The raindrops sure sounds so good on this tin-top house. This rain is making your boss horny. My naive Bessie, do you hear the rain on top of us?' I said, 'Yes, sir.' Ole Mule is going to rain inside of my sweet coochie. My own daddy was so bold that he told me I could not sleep in my bed while Mother is in the hospital. Poppy said, 'Your place is on Mattie's side of my bed. I am enjoying your heat. Mattie can't satisfy me like I need her to do.' He said, 'Damn, you are so good in bed. I mean I love to keep it in the family.'

He sucked my breast so hard the nipples were red and sore. Emma, my daddy molested, raped, and physically abused me until the rain stopped hours later.

"The sixth day he asked, 'Are you all right?' I nodded. 'Yes, sir.' Smiling, he said, 'You're damn right you are all right, your young tender coochie is adjusting well. It knows who it belong to: good ole Mule. All right, I have locked this front door. We are going to feed the hogs and come back and get in bed. I don't want a certain noisy neighbor coming over here interrupting my lovingmaking.

"Come now, Bessie, I am not leaving you here for Ella to chat, getting in my business. We are going to feed the hogs.' We went to the hog pen. He fed all the livestock. He walked up behind me and said, 'Come, sweet Bessie, I have something for you.' I was playing with the pigs. Mule said, 'I am going to teach you a lesson in farming. Today, you don't have time for those pigs.' He took my hand and led me over to the barn. Grinning, he said, 'Miss Bessie, I understand these animals better than most folk. When I lived in the country, we raised cows. Our neighbors raised sheep. I help them, fed, and cared for their flock of sheep. They had a batch of new females. I picked me one young female sheep to pet and treat special. She was one year old. The old farmer told me these groups of lambs were ready for breeding. They range from ten to twelve months old. We will do the breeding next week when I get back home. The ole farmer was gone for a week end. They asked me to feed the livestock. I fed the herd and took my sheep into a separate little shed far away from the herd so they could not hear her. I have always been big for my age. I put the young lamb in a small pen where she could not get away from me. I fucked that young tender sheep a long time. It felt so good. That lamb was groaning like a human being. That turned me on. That made me feel very macho and powerful as I rammed all of ole Mule inside that soft lamb. My young lamb was trembling as she took it all. I finished and left. I could hear her moaning as I proudly left her lying on the hay.

"'When I came back the next evening I noticed the young lamb was bloody. I cleaned her up, hugged her, and petted her. She stopped trembling and relaxed after a while. This time I sat my special lamb down in my lap on top of my dingdong . . . Ole Mule got a tight hug on the lamb and held it in place. The lamb could not get away from me. I forced this big dingdong in the young lamb as she tremble and moaned. After about ten minutes, I pushed and powered up very hard. Yes, Miss Bessie, I pushed my manhood all the way into the young sheep. She went ba-ba as I took what I wanted. Yeah, I socked this dingdong all the way up inside the young lamb until I felt her jewel. The soft lamb took every inch of me until she was sitting on my nuts. I fucked that baby female sheep until she collapsed. That scared ole Mule. I rushed out of the pen and laid the lamb down with her mama sheep. The lamb lay under her mama trembling, moaning and ba-ba-ba. Ole Mule came home like nothing had happen. The old farmer came home later that night.

"'He called me and said, "'Did you know what happened to my baby lamb?" I said, "'No, sir. They were all fine when I left last evening. What happened?" He said, "'Something got a hold of one of my lamb that was in heat. Her female organs were ripped and so torn the veterinarian had to put it to sleep." The old man said, "'I don't know how one of the old ramps could do that much damage." Mule smiled saying, 'I told the farmer I will be more careful the next time I am tendering your sheep.'

"Mule said, as he pulled me closer, 'I think I was too big for that poor little lamb. I didn't expect that to happen. I previously fucked one of the mama sheep, and she didn't die. I thought it would be a thrill to break the young lamb in.' I was trembling after Mule told me what happen to that lamb. This made me certain that he was crazy. Now his focus was me. He said, 'My innocent Bessie, you will need this first. He made me drink the corn liquor without the Kool-Aid. Things began to spin around. He laid me down on some hay and said, 'Let's leave the door open.' I asked, 'Why are we here, Daddy?' Mule said, 'I just looked at my male hog as I was feeding them a few minutes ago. That ole boar's dick was so big and hard it turned me on. I can't wait until we get back home.' This pervert grabbed and stripped my dress off. He was making loud noises as he sucked my breast. I said, 'Please be quiet, I don't want anyone to hear this.' 'Oh no, Miss Bessie, we must be heard.' He said, 'Okay, little gal, just watch what happens.' He bent me over a pile of hay. Mule ripped my panties off and began ramming me. He forced his oversized penis in my butt. He looked out toward the hog pen and yelled. 'Listen at your master, all you gilts. You will be fucked tonight just like this. I want my boar to hear Ole Mule riding his heifer. I brought you as close as possible so my hogs can smell your fresh hot pussy. I need my boar hogs to smell you. I want them to hear how I make you scream as I fuck you.'

Mule was grinning as he said, 'Listen, listen, sweet Bessie. They heard me sucking you now. The sounds and smell is working.' I could hear the hog making loud noises. Mule said, 'The whole pen of hogs smells us now. My come has a loud odor. Listen, they are grunting and rooting. We got them stirred up. I want my hogs to hear you scream like you have been doing every day and night I am up in you. Bessie, I need you to give it to me little hot, heifer.' He rammed so hard I screamed. He yelled, 'That's it, Bessie, let them know Ole Mule is fucking his new coochie.'

"Mule withdrew his penis out of me and leaned back. This time he turned around with his butt on my back. He was facing the hog pen. The jarring was different. I screamed, 'You have just torn up my rectum.' He said, 'That's good, baby, I am going to need you to moan and scream a little louder. Let me hear you, sweet Bessie.' Now fear took over. I moaned scream and hollered. Mule said, 'Louder, bitch. Louder, bitch. I want the hogs to hear you moan, groan, and scream as I am fucking you. Louder, my hot bitch.' I moaned and hollered until he filled me up several times.

"This time it felt like someone had rammed hot lava in my rectum. 'I got to hear that sweet moan like you did last night, Miss Bessie, two more times and I will let you up. I know that my ole boar hog will smell my hot pussy and get harder than a rock. We are stimulating our two boar hogs.' Mule was grinning as he said I felt sorry for the young female pigs tonight. 'Those boars of mine will fuck every sire in the pen this evening. Our hot fucking episode will let them know I am the baddest male on this farm. Ole long-dick Mule is in charge on my farm . . . I need them to hear me popping this hot pussy, my innocent Bessie.' It was then that I realized this man is very crazy. He is a sexual predator. Mule yelled out, 'Hey, Mr. Boar, I want you to know I can fuck this coochie just as long as I want to. I won't get stuck like you.' I don't know how long he used my body. I guess until I could not stand it any longer. I remember going into a daze with my daddy's dingdong inside of me. I don't know how long he used my body. Hours later, I woke up in bed. He kissed me on my forehead and said, 'I will always cherish this time we are having together. We have done some unforgettable things together. Sweet Bessie, we have made many hot sexual memories. I bet those hog will never forget us either. You should be happy, little gal. I let you rest after I brought you home. You have slept half of the night. I am ready to fuck again.' Trembling, I said, 'My vagina is injured so badly inside. Could we wait until tomorrow?' 'No, there is not a chance, little chili pepper.'

"He smiled and said, 'Because I just got acquainted with this little, hot box, I must get in it every chance we get. We cannot waste any time while my old lady is out of my way. Poppy can't stay out of it. I don't know what I am going to do when Ole Mattie comes home. This coochie is so good, I can't dream of living without it. Who knows . . . I might send her home to see her old aunt. They can take care of her until she gets better. I think that is what I will do. I can take care of you and enjoy my new treasure.' The week went on. I was trapped. He continued molesting me, regardless of my agony. My body was in misery. My body was so raw, I stayed at home two days out of school. It was so bad I was not able to go to see my mama.

"That Friday, I got enough strength to go to school. I was so scared that Poppy would come home early and molest me again. I thought school would be a safe place for a little while. My homeroom teacher asked why I was so sad. She said, "I thought you were worried about your mother's sickness." I said, "No, that is not the reason I was crying.' I told her I was scared of my daddy. Sobbing, I said, 'Mule has raped and molested me the last ten days and nights while my mother is very sick in the hospital.' The lady asked, 'Who is Mule?' I said, 'My daddy.' I went on and told them that one day he came home early. He raped and physically abused me from lunchtime that day until late that night. He was so drunk on that Friday night, he pee all over himself and fell asleep with his big leg across my thighs. There was no way for me to get up from under him. I was so alone and helpless. Tears washed the paper I was writing on. The teacher started to cry. She said, 'Don't worry.' She took me into the office.

"She began to write. After I told her what happen. She got up and led me to the principal's office. She asked me to tell the principal my story. I was shaking. I said, 'I can't retell it. I am so ashamed. Please, Mrs. William doesn't think I am a bad girl.' Mrs. William passed the long yellow pad to the principal. He said, 'No, young lady, I do not feel anything but anger and disgust.' Mr. Sampson got up and yelled, 'I can't believe a man would do this to a child. Is this your stepfather or your mother's boyfriend?' I dropped my head and said, 'No, he is my blood father.' He came close to me and said, 'We will protect you. I must call the police.'

"The policeman brought a nice woman with them. They took me to the hospital first. A few hours later, the doctor came in and told the social worker, 'This child is full of semen. Her rectum is so torn that we will do surgery in the morning. More x-rays are needed to see the extent of her injuries. You can plainly see the injuries on her young body.' The doctor said, 'We are going to give you something for pain and inflammation.' I was there five nights. It was a nightmare. The nurses, doctors, case manager, and social workers were so kind to me. Yet I was afraid Mule would find and kill me.

"They did a rape kit on me. The nurse put medicine on a few torn places on my arm. She asked me, 'How did you get the bruises on my arm and legs?' Crying, I said, 'Mule dragged me across the wooden floor and my legs and arms were torn by the wood in the barn.' I said, 'Poppy was throwing me around when I tried to stop him.'

"He threatened to kill me. I was assigned to a physician, therapist, and psychologist. They discharged me from the hospital. My new case manager took me to a safe nice home with an elderly lady. They told me I would be safe there. The police said, 'I bet your daddy will not call and make out a missing person report.'

"My new foster parent was a strong lady. Her name was Mrs. Henrietta. They had moved me to the opposite side of town. Two months after I moved, we went to the doctor. They updated my tetanus and immunization shots. The nurse took tubes of blood and a urine sample. The doctor told Mrs. Henrietta, 'We got a problem.' She asked, 'What is wrong?' The doctor said, 'This child is pregnant. The sheriff department will have to get involved. Do not let her father anywhere near her.' Mrs. Henrietta said, 'I am able to protect my house. I have a permit for my gun. He doesn't know where she is. I lived there for one year.'

"When we went to court, I urinated on myself when I saw Mule's face. My mother was not there. She was not allowed to come. Mule hired a lawyer that told the court I was mentally ill. He also said he had caught me with a boy from school. He did not know the boy's name. He had two older deacons from the church to testify on his character. I could not look up at those old men trying to make Mule be this respectable church leader and make me be the tramp.

"The prosecutor submitted letters from Mrs. Ella and another neighbors. They wrote a letter saying that they saw my daddy raping me in the kitchen. The judge read the letters. He asked me to read them. He asked me, if I knew these ladies. I said, 'Yes, sir. I have known them all of my life.' The judge said, 'This is the worst case I ever had.' The neighbors fear for their lives. This is the only way they will testify in two sworn depositions. They all feared Mule. The prosecutor called on the teacher and the hospital staff that took care of me. They proved that I was sane. The judge told the lawyer I did not need to testify. I was too scared.

77

Mule was fined $1,000 and sentence to five years' probation. He had to pay for the birth of my son. The judge told Mule he would go to prison for ten years if he ever came near me or call me.

"That was five years ago. I joined another church. Finally, a few months ago, the minster reached out to me and said they were sorry. 'The members love you and want you to come back to your home church. We will protect you while you are here.' I was afraid at first. After a few more months of therapy, I realized I must be strong enough to live with him dominating my life. Emma, I have a permit for my gun. I went to classes and passed with flying color. I am no longer afraid of Mule.

"Mule has lost all of his power in this church. My mother does not know the truth, and he will not let us visit together. He volunteered to clean the church just to keep face. That's the reason why my mother, Mule, and you must sit at least five hundred feet away from me. Mule has never bothered me since. Emma, just be safe." We held on to each other. She whispered in my ear, "You better get back home before Poppy comes looking for you. He will have a fit if he knows I am talking to you."

When I got home, Poppy was sleep. Granny was watching television. She smiled and asked, "Did you have a good time?" I said, "Yes, Granny, I enjoyed myself."

Now Bessie and I share a strong bond. This dark secret of our family makes me ashamed. The disgrace I felt would not let me tell Bessie how Poppy had tried to molest me. I escaped, she didn't. Bessie's mother, and my Granny, lives with a monster.

Emma

Many nights later, I had nightmare about Mule hurting Aunt Bessie.

If this man could hurt his own daughter, what would he do to me? I decided I was going to hide me a knife. If he tried to hurt me again, I was going to kill him.

One day in our health class, they showed us a self-defense film. It showed if you stab a man in his groin or his nuts, the injury will stop the attack. This promise I made to myself, I am going to get even with this evil man. He has brought dishonor to the women in our family. From this day, I have to hide this secret.

One day Jake and Grandma were sitting on the porch as always. He brought grandma a box of her favorite Garret snuff. She stuffed her lips with snuff and smiled. She was so cheerful enjoying her snuff. Grandma spat into her little can. This was one of the few times outside of church she was content. Dipping snuff was her happy time. She loved Jake like he was her son. Grandma trusted him with any and everything she had including me.

They were telling joke and talking about back in the day. Jake's grandmother and my grandmother grew up together down in the town of Gagger. They began to sing the song his grandma had taught him before she died a few years ago. On this day, he brought Grandma some old pictures of his mother and grandma when they were girls. Granny said, "Lord, Lord, I remember those sandy valleys in West Alabama. We farmed the land as share croppers. My mama and daddy worked the same land until they died. When ole master died, his son sold the land we had to move here. It was scary leaving a place where you grew up and believed that, you would die there. It was a good place to raise your family. This forced us to go back to our roots and live independently.

"I am glad we moved here. I married a hardworking man. He works at the foundry. We got a new kind of life now. We don't have to depend on the crop to live. We get a paycheck every week my husband works. He has never taken a day off since he had the job. He might get drunk and sometimes beat me, but he is a good provider. I love that black man. He is all I have." Granny went on to say, 'One day your granddaddy was sober and in his good mind . . . He told her that his daddy told him, "You got to whip your woman's ass to let her know who the boss is." This made me sad. I know Mule is the boss. I never disobey him, I don't know why he will still beat me. We have been together thirty years and he still needs to let me know he is the boss." I felt bad for my grandma. She was totally dependent on my Poppy. She made $10 a week cleaning the white folks' house for the last fifteen years. Now she is too old, they told her. The family needs a young gal that can move fast and get more work done for the money.

Granny was staring out across the field. She said, "The last five years I just kept the house, farm, my garden, and raised my great-granddaughter. That's all an old woman like me can do." She closed her eyes and started humming. In a little while, she was sleep. Jake went home early. I woke grandmother up and said, "Let's go to bed." Jake came by as he usually did the next evening. He smiled and said, "Come saddle up, Miss Emma. Just like ole time." Smiling, he pulled me farther back in the saddle. My back was against his chest. I said, "I don't want to sit back so far." He said, "You are too big to sit on the edge of the saddle. Please come over here, Emma, I want you to trust me and just relax. Do you want to ride your horsey today?" I hesitated. He reached out for my hand. "Oh well, missy, do you want your candy today. Here it is now. Sit back and enjoy your evening ride." My horsey started rocking as I rode. I said, "Horsey, I don't like this ride. I want to get off my horsey." Jake said, "Okay, I think we will go back to your bike rides a few times since you are complaining about your horsey rides are rough. See what I mean, little girl? Just sit back and glide on your bicycle." I did what he said. We played riding the bicycle for two weeks. I had fun. This was my playtime on the bike. I learned to relax. He smiled and said, "There are no children close by, so I come to let you have a little fun every day. Are you saying you don't like to have fun every day with me?" I smiled and said, "Yes, sir, I do like having fun with you."

It was Friday night; great-granddaddy was gone to get drunk. Grandma asked Jake to bring her some gin. She said, "I need my tottie on Friday night so I will be sleep when Mule comes home drunk." On this night, Jake made Grandma her favorite drink: gin and tonic. The radio was playing the blues. Grandma said, "I like Ethel Waters. They don't play her records like they used to. That black woman sings the truth for Negro women." Jake smiled and said, "That is fine for you ladies, but I prefer BB King. His music says what a black man is feeling." The music played louder tonight. After a while, Grandma nodded off to sleep. Jake smiled and asked me, "Do you like the blues, Emma?" I said no. "My favorite song is 'I was dancing with my darling to the Tennessee Waltz.' I really like that song." Jake snapped, "I don't like that song, it is not for poor folk. That song is for rich folk." I said, "I still like it." Jake said, "I also like, Howling Wolf, 'Back Door Man.' Most of all, I love John Lee Hooker 'Roadhouse' Muddy Waters' songs. My favorite is 'I Am Your Hoochie Coochie Man.'" He stared to sing "I Am Your Hoochie Coochie Man." Yeah, baby, he is singing about me. No, Sir Jake did not sing church songs to me tonight, he was singing the blues. This evening was very different. He finished that song and started to sing "Ain't She Fine." I was enjoying the music. He said, "Come, big girl, and get your last ride of the night." I said, "No, thanks." He looked sad. "Oh, come on, so I can go home. Let's take it easy and just glide along." This was a nice easy ride. Slowly it changed. The bike ride started pushing against my bottom. This really hurt. I struggle. "What is that?" He smiled and said, "That's just ole Bo giving his big girl her last ride of the night." I don't know why he kept on singing. Then he stopped singing and started grunting. "We are going to change up for the end of the day. Your horsey is getting jealous. Your horsey thinks you don't want to ride anymore." I smiled and said, "Oh no, I still like riding my horsey."

"Okay, let's ride, Miss Emma." This ride was smooth and easy. A little while later the horsey took off and the ride was fast and bumpy. He was panting. Mr. Brown was breathing so hard. He said, "Your stallion is hot and sweaty coming into the home stretch." I said, "Something is wrong with this saddle the stick hurts me again." I hopped up and ran in the house.

Oh my goodness, I looked down and saw blood on my dress. What happened, my period was coming on? I was embarrassed. I was moaning in pain. I never had this much pain on my period. I cleaned myself up. There was something slimy in the blood on the rag. I didn't know what it was. Tonight, I was so confused.

Why am I hurting so on my period? What just happened to me? Riding my horsey so rough has made my period come on early. My panties got soggy while I was riding the horse. I am glad I had good panties on; they protected my private area. I am glad I kept my dress down while I was riding. It protected me from bleeding on Jake. I don't know what happened.

After my bath, I did like Grandma taught me to do. I put a Kotex on when my period start. This period really hurt so badly. This night, I went to bed feeling shame. I was so embarrassed because my menstrual had started on my horsey. I was so humiliated I didn't go back outside. I sang myself to sleep. I wish my mama was here. I bet she would stop my horsey from rocking me so hard.

The next few days when Jake came around, I went in the house and did not talk to him. He had proved to me he was not my friend. My horsey should not hurt me like that making my period come early. Mr. Brown sat outside and sang with Grandma. Granny asked, "What's the matter, Emma?" I said, "Nothing. I just want to sit inside by myself." Jake didn't say anything at first. Then he said to Granny, "That little gal is sure growing up fast. It won't be long and she will be out on her own like a young woman." I was very mad. He doesn't know what I like. I don't want to be a big girl out on my own. I love living with my loving granny. Why does he keep talking about me being a young woman?

It was a new year for me at school I was in the seventh grade. Now we started changing classes. No longer would I stay in the same room with the same teacher. We changed classrooms and teachers. It was exciting. I was doing the preteen classes. Granny and I made clothes for me all summer so that I would have a new wardrobe. My loving granny is so proud of me in school now.

September finally arrived. I wore my new clothes to school with pride. It was great wearing a two-piece outfits I made for myself. Granny made me ten new outfits over the summer. Now it is fall. I receive so many compliments on my new clothes. The first five outfits were perfect. We had been in school two months. My clothes drew up. Granny said we got to be careful using too much hot water. This would cause the clothes to shrink. Now some of my clothes were fitting me too tight. I had to let the seam out. Granny said, "We made your clothes in the early spring, now it is fall and you have grown out of them." She adjusted the seam so my clothes would fit me nicely.

This quarter of school was great. I got new friends and new teachers. I made As in all my class. My class was exciting as we prepared for October Fest. I made myself an outfit just for the Festival. I got so many compliments on my outfits.

When the cold weather came I went into the big cedar wardrobe to get clothes from last winter. Grandma said, "You cut that dress too small." I said, "No, ma'am, I cut it by the pattern you made for me." My skirts were fitting so tight I had to move the seam and loosen the skirt. I stopped eating a lot. One day in physical education I got sick. I threw up all my food. The teacher took me home and told my grandma to take me to the doctor. There is a virus going around in the school.

The next day we rode the bus to town. The nurse told me to urinate in the cup I did not know what she meant. The nurse smiled and said pee-pee in the cup. The doctor checked me gave me a prescription and told us they would call when the lab work came back. A few days later we got the call and returned to the doctor's office. Dr. Robertson looked at my grandma and said, "This gal is pregnant." Grandma jumped up and said, "It can't be true, Doctor. That has to be a mistake this child don't go anywhere I am not with her. Emma is not around any little boys. I keep my eyes on my big baby. I am with her at all times. No, sir, that got to be wrong." I started to cry. I didn't understand. What happened to me? When did it happen? I was crying and felt so alone and humiliated. How could I be pregnant? Whatever that mean don't apply to me. It's got to be a mistake.

That evening, Jake came by. My grandma told him, "Let's step outside." She was very mad. I heard her yell at Jake. He didn't come in the house on this day. The next morning, I was getting ready for school. Grandma said, "Never mind school. Just wait a minute." Someone knocked on the door; it was Jake. He had a sneaky look on his face. "Are you ladies ready? Here is the package you told me to pick up, Mrs. Mattie." Grandma said, "Give us a few minutes." Granny gave me the package. She told me to wear the new dress. I didn't know why I had to dress up. Granny smiled and said, "You look pretty, so let's go." He drove up to the courthouse. I didn't want to go in. Grandma said, "Git in here, gal. It is too late to say no now." The lady asked my name, I said Emma. She asked, "How old are you?" I said, "I am twelve years old." The clerk asked me, "Who is this with you?" I said, "My great-grandma." She asked Granny, "Where is this child's parents?" No one said anything. I looked down and said, "I don't know. I live with my great-granddaddy, my Poppy." The clerk asked my granny, "Do you give permission for this gal to get married?" I was in shock. Grandma said, "Yes, ma'am." I don't remember anything else. When she finished the ceremony, Jake reached over and held my hand. He said, "You belong to me now, gal. Yes, sir, you belong to me." I started to cry. The tears would not stop. Grandma was sniffling too. We rode home in silence. She said,

"Come on, gal. This time she held my hand and said, "I didn't mean for this to happen to you." Grandma went into the house. "We need to hurry before your poppy gets here." Somebody might get hurt. I followed her. She walked into my room. She hugged me crying . . . She said, "You don't live here anymore. I packed you a bag." I said, "Why, Grandma? I don't want to stay with Jake. Why are you making me go with him? He is a man, and I am just a twelve-year-old child." She shook her head and said, "When I realized that Jake was the only man coming around here, I confronted him. It broke my heart to know I had trusted this man around you, and he had taken advantage of an innocent child like you. No one could make me believe that Jake would trick me like this.

"When your mama left you, I became your protector. Believe me I thought I was doing a good job. Lord, please, have mercy on us—what a mess. I felt safe with that boy around. He said he was our guardian. Once or twice a week he would say, 'I will kill anybody if they mess with you, Mrs. Mattie and little Emma.' I haven't slept well since the doctor told me you were pregnant. You are my innocent great-grandbaby. This misguided trust has cost you your future. You were going to be my big schoolteacher. I saw you playing school with your doll and your little stuffed black puppy. It was hard to understand. I never saw you playing with the boys your age. I only saw you play with the girls a few times. I went over and over again in my mind trying to figure this pregnancy out. Finally, I called ole slick Jake out. Oh yes, he is a slick one. I was hot with him. If the truth be told, I wanted to kill him. He had deceived me. I called him outside and asked him, 'How could you do this to us?' He didn't deny it yesterday. No no, he had that slick grin on his face. He said it with pride, 'If she is pregnant, it is mine. This whole ordeal has made me sick. My chest has been hurting ever since. Oh well, baby, we can't change what has happened. We must learn to live with this mess."

"Please, please, Grandma, don't make me go with Jake. I wanted to tell you the night he hurt me while I was riding the horse. I was sitting on my horsey. That night the horse was wild. It was a rough ride. Jake had a stick in his lap that hurt me. I told him to take that stick out of his pocket. I didn't like the way it felt. Jake said the stick was

4

part of the new saddle. Smiling, he said, 'Let Ole Bo gets rid of that ole stick.' He told me to stand up. I did. He adjusted it I guess. A few minutes later, he pulled me back down on the saddle and said, 'Okay, little girl, I have move the stick from the middle of the saddle. This will be a smoother ride. I guarantee it.' Jake whispered, 'Remember, Emma, you got to get used to riding in your new saddle.' I said okay. I didn't feel the stick anymore. He restarted the ride slow and easy. This was the longest and warmest ride ever. Later the horsey got faster and hotter. The horsey was panting. Jake was sweating, and he yelled, 'Enjoy your ride, little girl.' At the end of the ride he asked, 'Wasn't that fun?' I said, 'I guess so.' To this day, I was confused then and now I am still confused.

"Mama, you are all the mother I ever had. Please, I need you to believe in me I didn't do anything wrong . . . You were always here with me. There has never been a time I was alone with Jake, except at the hog pen. He did not touch me at the hog pen. Every time I was on the horsey, you were there. I had my clothes on when I rode the horse. You saw me riding my horsey, remember, Grandma?

"Granny, please explain how I can be pregnant. The big mystery for me is when did Jake get inside of my body? How did a baby get inside of me? You were always there. Grandma, did you know how Jake did this awful thing to me. How did he do it right in your presence? Why did this take place in me? I can't understand how it happened. The only other thing I can remember that was different was you were nodding after you ate your treat that evening. I remember another particular evening Jake rode me on my horse so long and hard he sweated on my dress. I got up wet from his sweat. That was the time I wanted to tell you about it. The next time it happened, I was so embarrassed because my period started in Jake's lap on that long, hard horse ride. I knew you trust him in my mind. I thought you knew about breaking in a new saddle, I suppose. Grandma, I thought if I complain about training on a new saddle, you would be upset with me . . . You said it was okay to ride my horse. We sang 'She be coming around the mountain when she come' so many verses. I dropped off to sleep. My horsey rode me very slow and easy. When

I woke up, Jake said, 'You sure enjoyed this ride. Your horsey rocked you to sleep.' I got up my dress was wet from Jake's sweat.

"This cunning man was as happy as he said, 'Ole Bo must train you for your new saddle.' That was a painful experience as we broke in the new saddle on my horsey. This stupid horsey game got me in this mess. I don't want to leave home, Granny. Please let me stay. I will be a good girl."

We sat on my bed for a while just crying together and holding each other. "Please tell me how this could be possible. You are always with me. I only played here at home right here on the front porch. There was never a time I went anywhere by myself. I need you to believe me, please help me, Granny. Don't make me go with Jake."

Granny took me by my hand. She led me out of my room and walked over to Jake and gave him my hand. "I loved you great-grand-baby, but you got to go with Jake and do what he say. He is now your husband. You belong to Jake now. You must do what he tells you to do . . . Just be obedient to him like I am to your great-granddaddy. He got a good job. He will work and take care of you and that baby."

That word *baby* rocked my world. I hated the sound of the word. The mere idea that a little person is growing inside of me scared me. My world is upside down now. I have never had sex with a man. I can only remember that I am a young twelve-year-old girl. I should not be pregnant. Today, I see Jake as a con artist. He has just played a game on the two of us. He used my grandmother's isolation to befriend her. He pretended to be my friend. He never wanted my friendship. He wanted my innocence. Neither one of us ever suspected any foul play. He used playtime and singing time to do his dirty work.

Jake Brown should be put in jail for what he has done to me. How and when did this man take advantage of my body I don't know? He is the age of my dad. Now here we are. He pretended to be a family friend. Oh yes, he has slicked his way into my childish body. Grandma said his house is now my home. "Just remember how I trained you to cook and clean. You know how to can your own vegetables. Whatever you don't know how to do, ask me. It's a shame you just had your twelfth birthday. God knows you are just a baby yourself. Go ahead now, get out of here." I held Granny's hand. She led me to Jake's car.

Jake walked up to Granny and said, "This is for Mule, I gave you yours when we left your house going to the courthouse this morning. Do you know what you did with it, Mrs. Mattie? You were so upset.' Granny was crying; she said, "I am still hurt and disappointed. Yes, I put the envelope away in my cedar chest." Granny looked in the envelope and said, "I pray this will satisfy Mule." Jake smiled and said, "Yes, Mrs. Power, I double what he said his asking was. He will be fine. When we leave, look in your card and you will see I gave my new Granny-in-law double the asking. That's our secret." Mr. Brown winked his eye and walked around his car.

He opened the door for me. I sat down in Mr. Brown's car. I was lost, sad, and scared. He got in the car smiling. Before he started the car, he reached over and peeked under my dress. Just look at all of this rubbing my stomach. Jake had this sly grin on his face and said, "We got you now. Mrs. Emma, Jake Junior, and I have you all to ourselves. All this is now mine."

Jake Brown drove his car to the colored café; he bought two dinners. He whispered to the owner. She smiled and said congratulations. She gave us a little rainbow cake. This new husband of mine was old enough to be my daddy. He is here smiling and grinning, while I am crying inside.

When we got to his house, he sat the food on the porch. He picked me up and carried me inside. Grinning, he said, "Welcome to your new home, Mrs. Emma Brown." He went back and got the food. "Well, girl, this is your new home. I picked up some flowers for you." I said, "That's nice. I like roses." "Hmm," he said.

My granny said when a person gives you a rose it means you are not common. Your are unusual, choice, rare or unique. She said a rose has the best fragrance in the world. It brought a smile to Granny's face as she said Carol is the white girl I raised. That child loves me. The day I retired she brought me six roses. Water came in Granny's eyes, as she said Carol's precious gift touched my heart, I will never forget my special day. My Emma never forget the power of a rose. The smell of those red roses finally made my granny feel unique. She still has those rose petals in her Bible." Mr. Brown smiled and said, "Your young tender body smells like a rose. Oh yes, it does. I carried the smell of your sweet rose on me every night the last two years."

"On my twelfth birthday I receive a yellow rose from my friend at the curb market. Granny told the lady she wanted me to have my first rose on this special birthday. That was the last year, I could be a girl. Next year I will be a teen." Jake smiled and said, "Girl, that ain't the kind of flower we colored folk like. A rose flower is for the rich white folk. We common people like lilies, honeysuckles, and daises. Let me put your daises in this fruit jar. You can be proud of your new home. This is one of the best living rooms set in the community. Here . . . come and sit down on your new couch." Quietly we watched his black-and-white television in the living room. Later, he said, "Come on, let me show you your new house. Here is your kitchen. This is our bedroom. I took my half bath on the back porch and made it bigger with a bathtub. There are only a few colored people with a bathtub inside in this whole town. Look around at your own kitchen. Yes, Mrs. Emma Brown, you are a woman now with your own house. Ha-ha I told your granny you would soon be out on your own. She just didn't know like I knew. Just look at you now. You got a husband, baby, and your own house. Look in the stove. I have a few pots and pans. We can go shopping Saturday. Why are you looking so sad, girl? I am a good catch. Many women wanted me. Ever since I laid eyes on you, I wanted you." I started to cry. Sniffing, I said, "You tricked me. I wanted to go to school. I dreamed of being a teacher. Now I am pregnant and my life will never be the same. My friend can go on dates and stuff, and now I am stuck here with you. This is not fair to me at all. This is all about what you wanted. All of your stuff does not make me happy. I want to go back go to Granny and sleep on my own bed. You only have one bed, Mr. Brown. Where am I going to sleep? I have never slept with anyone but my granny. I am not going to sleep in a bed with a man. That is not right. I want to sleep on the couch tonight." He snatched me up and said, "Okay, that's enough of that little girl pipe dream. Today, you became part of me. That means you are mine. You will sleep with me in my bed. Come on, baby, act nice to ole Jake." He led me to the bedroom. "Be good to me, baby, I'll be good to you. We are husband and wife now. I have been waiting for this a long time. Tonight, my bed will become our bed." Jake was grinning; he said, "Men around here call me Bo. Ha-ha, little girl, you will find out later." Jake continued to boast. He said, "I bet the young bucks that been looking and wanting you at school didn't know what happened. I simply outfoxed those young bucks trying to get up in this. I played it close to the vest. Yes, I played close to your great-grandma's breast and got the prize. You are my young pretty innocent gal. I got you, now all to myself. I don't have to pretend to your granny anymore. I got her in my pocket. Yes, sir, I got her in my pocket. I know your value. Mule was bragging about what he was going to get for you. The ole man told me you are prime meat. He was right. I double the amount he was going to ask for. I am damn sure Mrs. Mattie could get some benefits from all her long hard hours taking care of my prize. That's what I am talking about. Knowing what you want and know how to get it is the way a fox operate. When I was a young man, the ole men in the country called me fox—yes, sir, I am a smart fox . . . Mule didn't get a chance to test this out.

"When Mrs. Mattie told me I had to marry you. This made me so happy, I was smiling from ear to ear. I rushed and bought this little lace dress. She told me to buy a size 14. I noticed your little belly was sticking out your clothes a few months ago. I did not say anything to anybody. I wanted to be on the safe side, so I bought a 16, and it is just right. I love the way it fits. You are a pretty bride today. Mrs. Emma, you are as pretty as a blooming new rose.

Never forget, young girl, Big Bo takes what he wants. You should know that by now. I wanted you, and look where you are. Now I got you right where I wanted you, I was trembling." He said, "Stand up, my princess, and let me help you out of your wedding dress. You like it, don't you?" Grinning, Jake said, "I picked a dress with a zipper in the back so I could slip you out easy." Trembling, I said, "I have never been naked before a man, Mr. Brown." He walked behind me and said, "I know." Jake unzipped my dress, pulled the shoulders off, and my new dress fell to the floor. Now I was standing before this man with just my underwear on. "Mrs. Emma, the rest of these clothes must come off. Here we go. This is your new honeymoon nighties. It is short and sexy." He put the fancy top on me. I said, "I don't feel comfortable in something this short." He smiled and said, "You are so pretty in that sassy nighty." I asked, "Where is the bottom that goes with this nighty set?" "Why, Mrs. Brown?" He smiled and said, "This is all you can wear now. Matter of fact, I will not allow you to wear any panties around our house for a long time. I will only permit you to wear panties when our baby gets your belly bigger, and I need panties to protect him. Otherwise, I want you free and available whenever I want to get in there. Please remember again the rule: you cannot wear any panties in my house." He glided across the room and turned on the radio. Etta James was singing "My Love." Smiling, he said, "That's my song." I murmured to myself, "You are not my love, ole goat." He was dancing, dragging me around the room. "We have so much to learn. I will teach you how to dance later." He said, "You look so puzzled. What is wrong, Mrs. Emma Brown? My dear child, today, I am transforming you from a girl to a woman. There is nothing anybody can do to me now. You belong to me. We are going to have a wonderful honeymoon." I said, "Yes, sir, Mr. Brown, first can you tell me how did a baby get inside my stomach?" He took my hand and said, "Well, you seem so confused. I am going to break it down for you. This is how it all went down. Shh . . . shh . . . this is my little secret I kept from Poppy. He thought he was smarter than me, I proved him wrong. Okay, Mrs. Brown, let your husband explain. Let's start with your bicycle rides. I had you to sit to one side for a good reason. Your seat sat on my staff—really that is what ole Bo calls this mighty right hand.

"When you turned nine years old, I started giving you sour candy. Actually, I soaked your candy in sweet wine. You were so young, it did the trick. You would nod off while riding your bicycle. I was so happy to touch those fine soft thighs. My precious box lies between your soft thighs. It took a while for you to get used to it and relax.

"Your little legs would dangle in the air as I massage your breast and stomach. Finally, after two years, I was able to touch the front of your tender body. Slowly, I introduced my staff inside your thick soft thighs. The first night I touched your tight hot box, I come on myself. I had to wait for you to go in the house before I could get up. I went home smiling and smelling my lucky hand. The aroma of your young rosy body became an obsession of mine. That was your early prep. When you turned ten, we started the horsey ride, remember, Mrs. Emma? It took me six months for me to get you comfortable straggling your saddle. Remember how I pulled you back on the saddle? My rod was your saddle. When you were riding your horsey, I could feel your little hot bottom relaxing and slowly open a little at the time. I loosened it up one ride at a time. Finally, the straddling paid off. I checked your bottom about six months ago, and to my surprise, your innocent vagina had loosened up much more than I expected. I continued using the same angles until it was wider. Ole Bo got so good I knew just how to slide inside of those little fancy open-legged drawers your granny bought. Once inside the panty, I would tilt you a certain angle that open you up. Then I learned how and when I could slide the tip in easy without you knowing what was happening. When you complained about the stick hurting you, I knew I had too much in you. I would pull back and kept riding you. I got news for you, little hot mama, you enjoyed the thrills those rides gave you. Sometimes I would work a whole week on a certain angle. Inch by inch I worked my way in through all that little fuzz. I always stopped immediately when you said the stick hurt you. Didn't I stop, sweet baby? When I worked on the plantation, Ole Boss said I love giving my young gals a pony. They learn to enjoy their ride. Most young white girls have their first orgasm on their pony. Ole Bo was a young boy on the farm that learns a lot about girls and women enjoying the ride. I did just what ole boss said. Ha-ha, that took skills. I needed those skills to get what I cherish the most that little cherry of yours between your legs. By the time you got used to the ride, it was all joy for me. My beloved innocent precious Emma, I enjoyed the wait as I rock you hard and harder until I loosened you up. Ole Bo is so big I had to prepare your body for this. I used those techniques I learned from the farm. It has been a big help. Early rides help me groom you. Actually, I loved grooming you. This took patience. It took two years of weekly rides to get you ready for your new saddle. After two years of preparing your body, I accomplished my goal. Six months ago, the hot heat in your body made me know it was ripe. I happily went exploring into your new forest.

"Poor little naive baby, you didn't have any idea what I was doing, but I did. I trained you right. Finally, it took a long hot summer to break you in to our new saddle. Once I was inside of you, I went fishing. I hooked it a little at a time." I looked up at him and asked, "How did you get me pregnant, Mr. Brown?" Tears washed my face. "Do you remember the stick in the saddle?" I said, "Yes, I do remember the stick on my horsey rides. I thought my period had started in your lap." "No, that was my dick tearing my way into your body." Hearing Mr. Brown's confession was so embarrassing for me. This big man lifted my head. He said, "Look up, little girl. Let me make this clear. I am good at what I do. I am going to give you a thrilling honeymoon. Just relax—this is the start of a new chapter of lessons in life.

"When I was I boy, we used to measure who could shoot their pee the farthest. I won every time. Some of the guys shot straight out. My big rod will shoot straight up every time." Jake stood in front of me smiling. "Mrs. Emma Brown, I am going to show you a lesson in biology in living color. Have you ever watch the rocket at Cape Carnival lift off on television?" I said, "Yes, sir, Mr. Brown. I like watching the rocket lift off." "Look up, innocent Emma. I must introduce you to ole Bo's missile. This big powerful dick is a rocket. My childish wife, are you still confused about your pregnancy?" I said, "Yes, sir. I still don't understand how a baby got inside me." "Look, my princess." He was holding something in his hand. "Jake will solve your mystery right now. Ole Bo will show you. Sit down in this chair, my sweet rose, open those pretty thighs wide." I was trembling. I asked, "Why?" Mr. Brown said, "My princess, I need to see my trophy." Slowly I opened my legs. He came over and massaged my stomach. Without making a sound, he kissed my vagina, saying, "Oh yes, baby. I need to smell my sweet rose between these legs. This sweet smell reminded me how I went home happy many nights with the aroma of your sweet juice on my hand. Just two nights ago, I went home and masturbated. Do you know what I mean?" I said, "No, Mr. Brown, I don't understand." He started rubbing his penis slowly, and then he speeded up. All of a sudden he yelled, "Yes, baby, this is it. Here is comes. They called this masturbating. Look, sweet Emma, at your big rocket. Here it comes, baby, just for you." A stream of thick white juice shot straight up out of Mr. Brown penis. He was laughing so loud. "Men call this come. When you see this white milk coming out of my dick, this is my manhood. This milk is the place where live semen live. My semen was shot up inside of your vagina and pierced your egg. The egg is what you pass when you have a period. Now our fertilized egg is our baby. Listen, Emma, I changed what I soaked your candy in from wine to gin on your twelfth birthday. At first you complained and said you don't like this candy. I added sugar the next time, and you sucked the candy pop until you fell off to sleep. I got the results I set out to get. Both you and Mrs. Mattie were napping. You and Granny got a good nap each evening I came by. Nap time gave Ole Bo time to invade Mrs. Mattie's sweet rose garden. Touching you gave me a hard on every evening. Ole Bo loves smelling this body of yours. Finally five months ago, I made it inside of you. I was so happy. There are not enough words to express how happy I was. I enjoyed playing inside your hot coochie. Five days a week, I enjoyed our evenings together as Ole Bo eased this big dick inside those open-legged drawers you were wearing. See, baby, when you rode your horsey, you were straddled on my dick. That made it easy for me to shoot straight up in your coochie. Don't look so sad. You wanted answers, I am giving you the truth. Just a little while ago you said you wanted to go back to school. Okay, this is your first class. Please listen up, young girl. Today I am giving you a lesson in biology. Ole Bo is also teaching you grown folk's language.

"Look, my sweet wife, you learned that this is a penis in school, right?" I said, "Yes, sir."

"Today, this penis has become your dick. I am introducing you to grown-folk talk. Look at this dick. It is a rocket shooting straight up. This is called the milk of life. It was my milk (come) that carried my sperm into your vagina." I gasped. Grinning, Mr. Brown said, "Sweet Emma, you have just seen for yourself how my dick is full of the white milk of life carrying my sperms. The good part for me is I made sure you enjoyed the ride very much. Ole Bo made you feel so good you didn't even struggled or know what happened. Your candy was soaked in a better brand of gin that night. You dozed off smiling. I kissed your cheek as you slept. On that night, you slept about two hours. I knew my candy was working well. At first you were smiling and dozed off while sucking your candy. When you started snoring, this old fox worked his magic."

Tears washed my face. I was so ashamed. Jake said, "This illustration should help you understand how I launch my baby inside you. Your little hot body had adjusted to the horsey ride I played around in you after you dose off many evenings. You smiled as I played. Once Big Bo knew I was inside, I was able to get a good portion of me inside my sweet honey box. I will never forget the look on your face. You were enjoying riding your horsey, baby, you were smiling and enjoying every minute that evening. Beloved, it was the night I gave your best ride. It was so good to me. Ole Bo had you so hot you had come several times that night. I had your coochie wide open. I enjoyed it as I got it good and wet. That is when your hot wet pussy was ready for your Ole Bo. I slipped this dick inside of you without a struggle. The old fox went for the precious prize. Oh yes, Mrs. Emma Brown, this is when Big Bo's sperms swam up and pierced your egg and created our baby . . . Now you know.

"Today it is official: I can put this entire big dingdong inside of you now without playing games. My big black drill opened the gate when I tore your hymen. Miss Emma, the blood was not your period that night. It was ole Bo tearing into his kingdom. That night, Ole Bo pierced your little tender hymen, baby. I will finish the job tonight on our honeymoon. Did they teach you about that in school?" I dropped my head and said, "No, sir." He smiled and said, "That's a damn shame. I am glad I am your first teacher.

"Well, Bo has just given you your first lesson about our new body. You know this body belongs to me now. Ha-ha, baby girl, don't you remember the evening the back of your dress was soggy wet." I yelled, "Oh my god, you saw that. I was so embarrassed. My period started right there while I rode my horsey."

"No, no, baby girl, that was not your period. That was my manhood. It saturated your little pretty dress. I got a little too greedy. I couldn't control myself. You smiled and said, 'Yes, sir.' We kept playing and riding until you felt the dampness. When you felt the sogginess on your bottom, that was my overflow. You hopped up and ran. It was too late. My seed went swimming upstream. Now I realized that was too much for your little body. I am sorry I was too greedy. So much for Mrs. Brown life's lesson.

"We got to get busy, Mrs. Emma. The Browns honeymoon is on now. Your granny said you were her sweet rose. Today you became my sweet rose. There is not a flower anywhere that smells as sweet as Mrs. Emma's Brown, my sweet rose."

Jake led me over to a chair, he sat me down. He turned the radio on the song playing was "My Girl." "Mrs. Emma Brown, you are my girl. Here is your first wedding present to my girl from me." Jake took my nighties off, smiling. My whole body was trembling.

"Why can't I keep this nightie top on, Mr. Brown?" "It will get in my way hot stuff." Shaking, I said, "You just put this set on me." He smiled and said, "I know. It has to come off." Now I am so afraid as I sat in the chair naked and scared. He said, "Relax, my young tender filly." His big hands were all over my body. I tried to get up. He held me in the chair with one of his big hands. Jake got on his knees in front of me. He kissed my face and continued the kissing on to my shoulders and arms. Quickly, he started at the top of each breast, making circles, kissing each breast until he reached each nipple. He held the nipple in his mouth. Now his tongue was playing with the end of my nipple. He smiled and said, "Look at them now. Your sweet tit tells ole Bo that his pussy is so ready. Look, Mrs. Emma Brown, both nipples are very hard. Here is another lesson. When a woman's nipples get hard, that notifies the man her body is ready to be fucked. Oh, that's a new word I will explain to you later. Just look at my new tits. They have been calling me to suck them for the last four months." He massaged my breast one at a time I was nervous. Once he finished, he took both breasts and pushed them together as they met in his mouth. Slowly Jake massaged my stomach with baby's lotion. He smiled and said, "This is nice." He got up and walked to the back of the chair. He said, "Stand up, Mrs. Brown." He began kissing my back down to my butt. He continued as he walked back around and sat me back down in the chair. He kneeled in the front of me again. He looked at me, saying, "I got you all hot and ready. Mrs. Emma, do you like the way, I make you feel?" Trembling, I said, "Yes, sir." He smiled and said, "I am going to make you scream in delight before high noon on your wedding day." Slowly he kissed my stomach. My body had never tingled before. I made sounds I never knew was in me. Jake's big hands were massaging my shoulders. His tongue caressed my stomach until he reached the bottom of my belly. Now, Mr. Brown's tongue was tantalizing my entire body. Now I see what he is doing. This man took control of my body. Slowly he moved down kissing the inside of my thighs. His big finger went around in circles playing inside of my vagina. He played with my clitoris. I felt my body stiffen up. I was holding my breath trying not to react to his touch. I couldn't help myself now. I was trembling. His sucking and playing inside made me feel good. Next he dropped his head between my legs and began to blow in my vagina. The teacher showed us a video about the way the vagina look, but she did not tell us how it would feel. I remembered in the film they said this part of the body is the clitoris. I didn't understand what she meant when she described it. Now I just learned that it makes me feel good. I asked him to stop over and over again because I didn't like him taking control of my body. I was trapped. Mr. Brown was holding me against my will. Mr. Jake's kisses excited my whole body as he played inside of me. I really don't know what he was doing. I said, "Please don't hurt me." He yelled, "You will love this hurt, baby." His head disappeared again. Soon I could not see his face. My pregnant stomach covered his head, but he tantalized me. I could feel my body tighten up my heart was beating fast. I started to tremble. I yelled, "Oh, my goodness, what is happening to me." My heart was beating fast. His tongue was moving fast. My body tightens up as hot liquid ran out of my vagina. I never felt this way before in my life. He lifted his head and said, "Mrs. Brown, I see you like it. You are my hot chili pepper. I can feel the heat down here. I have an announcement for Mrs. Emma Brown. You are roasting hot. Baby, you are so ready." I was speechless. Now my body felt like it opened up. He yelled, "Mrs. Emma, this is your first wedding gift from Ole Bo. Yes, mama, your pure innocent girl body is sizzling hot. Oh yes, your new husband just gave you your first orgasm. The way you are hollering lets me know Ole Bo knows how to thrill your pussy." I yelled, "Why you are calling my vagina pussy, Mr. Brown?" He peeked his head up from under my stomach and said, "This is what a man calls it, so from here on in, it is a pussy." I said I thought that was the name of a cat. He smiled and said, "That is right, you have a pussy. It is soft like a cat. Some men say the softness of your pussy reminds them of a cat, and it has another name: coochie. Do you get it, Mrs. Emma Brown?" He said, "When you are with other people it is your vagina. When I am with you, it is my pussy. Mrs. Brown, you have dug your little nail into my back while I thrilled my pussy. You know it's mine, all mine, now. When I feel those scratches on my back, this is my proof it is good to you, my young tender wife. This good feeling I am giving you tells me my coochie is ready for your big dick. This is what happens when a girl becomes a woman. I need to get you at your hottest. Then you will enjoy your husband's rod." Over and over again he made my body react like he wanted it to. He was in control of my body. Jake thrilled me and gave me five orgasms before he stopped. I hated being trapped here with this old man, but now Mr. Brown is in charge of me. I tried to resist. I can't get away. He was too big and powerful. He kept thrilling my body. I lost control. He made me feel so good. I screamed, "Yes, it feels so good, Mr. Brown. What are you doing to me?"

"Sh . . . sh . . . Ole Bo knows what I am doing. I am so big I must help you get prepared, little tender gal. Mr. Brown must have you well lubricated before I can enjoy my wife. All your juice will make it easy when I ride into my promised land. Now I got you feeling good, aren't you happy you got Ole Jake as your new lover?

"None of those young class mates know how to do what I do. This is better than riding your horsey, isn't it Mrs. Emma Brown? Wait until I thrill your coochie on this unbridled horsey ride. Look at you, Mrs. Emma You are too hot to stop now. You are ready, baby. I must get in the saddle and trot. I am ready to saddle up."

Jake picked me up and carried me to his bed. He gave me a small glass of juice. I began to drink the juice. He said, "No no, you got to sip it slow to really get the flavor." I drank some more. He said, "Slowly down your drinking. Let yourself go. Relax, my young filly." I said, "This juice is strong. It is making me feel funny." He said, "It's okay this is your wedding day. You are supposed to feel that smooth relax feeling. Here drink the rest of your wine, I mean juice. I brought us some very expensive Manizchez wine. Mrs. Emma, I need you to drink one more sip and we are ready to go riding. This juice will take the fear right out of your mind. Ole Bo knows how to prepare Mrs. Brown for her husband." I really didn't know what he was doing. His kisses started the feeling again. He slowly laid me down. I said, "Okay don't hurt me, Mr. Brown." I tried to get up. I said, "Please don't hurt me, Mr. Brown. I am not a woman. I am just a young tender girl you are going to hurt me. I don't want you to do this to me."

He yelled, "Oh yes, this little tight hole makes my ride super good. Just know your body belongs to me now." I yelled, "Get off of me now, Mr. Jake this is hurting me." "No, my innocent girl, I can't do that now. Right now Ole Bo must shoot some hot honey up to my baby." He pushed me backward again. I fell back on the bed. "Listen Emma I don't want to beat you like your granddaddy has trained Mrs. Mattie. It is not necessary to beat a woman to control her. I am setting the rule and you will not break my rules. Do you understand, Mrs. Brown? Settle down and let Ole Bo enjoys his wedding day." I cried, "I need time to get use to all these strange rules." He smiled and said, "I gave your body two years to get ready. This is the final phase of my training and molding your tender body to your rod." "Please slow down, let me get used to this. I have never let anybody touch me like this, Mr. Brown." He looked up at me and smiled, saying, "I know. I am the first." This ole man sucked my tender breasts harder. "Oh yeah, I been watching these firm tits for a long time. The last few months I noticed they kept getting bigger. I got happy. I thought you were going through a growth perk. I am glad I was wrong. This is better. Yes yes, this was my baby making your breast bud and spread. Ole Bo got to have them now. This big growth spark came from my baby growing inside of you. These luscious tits make me so happy. Your tits have been begging me the last four months. They said, 'I am ready, Jake, come and get me.' Just look at my big round brown babies now. Ole Bo is answering their call. Here I am, sweet juicy babies, I coming to suck you dry. I can handle every ounce you got. Today Ole Bo got the message. They are singing, 'I am all yours. Signed, sealed, and delivered, I am yours Mr. Jake Brown.

"My baby makes you glow with hot passion. Junior has started growing inside his mother's belly, as his daddy deposits warm honey in his mama. Be quiet and let me feel good like I made you feel good. This is a two-way deal. I make you feel good. You make me feel good. Just look at those juicy babies now. I don't have to share my big breasts with anybody until our baby come out and start sucking your milk. It is my time for chocolate milk. Feed me my love juice, Mrs. Emma." Jake stopped sucking me. He whispered in my ear, "I felt how your body responded when I made you come. I want the same when I am fucking you, Miss Emma." He climbed on top of me and rode me. He yelled, "I am riding this filly on our wedding day." After an hour or so, he lay on the bed and to rest. I saw blood on the sheets under me. I got mad all over again. It is very clear to me now.

That was not my period on that night when he hurt me. Today, he doesn't have to pretend anymore. Jake proved he doesn't care. He has finishing ripping into me. The molesting and rape continued many hours. Now it is dark outside. He was laughing as he boasted, "I just finished what I started at Grandma's house." Poor ole Granny she didn't have a clue. Now I realized all that bicycling and horse riding was a way for him to trick me and get what he wanted. This big hard log he is now ramming in me feels like that stick that kept poking me at Grandma's house. The only thing I still don't understand is how the stick got inside of me. I didn't realize his rod was inside of me because my horsey was rocking so much.

Now he smiled in delight as he continued massaging my breast. I tried to sit up, he pushed me back on the bed. His big strong body covered me again. Now his moves were different. He was no longer pushing against my bottom as I sat on my horsey at Grandma's house. Tonight, this ole man was on top of me. His weight was so powerful I could not get up. I couldn't move. He forced my legs open; grinning, he said, "Open the gate for Ole Bo, my young hot filly. I am going to ride from morning until midnight." Then Jake started pushing against my vagina again and again. Why does he keep saying, "Just let me get the head in"? I didn't know what he meant. He slowed down. I thought he was going to get up. Oh no, Jake pushed through the hairs around my privates and plunge his big rod into me. "Yes, my big baby Emma, I am going to fill up this little hot pussy with your own hard dick on our honeymoon. I yelled, "Stop, you ole dirty man." He continued to ram his big rod into me again and again. Jake yelled, "Git up horsey. Come on, Miss Emma, I am almost there. I believe I can get a little more of this big fat dick inside this hot coochie." He grunted very loud as he rammed his penis inside of my stomach. This pain deep inside made me knew he had torn something loose inside of me. I am speechless. I fainted; I don't know how long I was unconscious. Finally, I came to myself. He was still moaning and grunting. I remembered him saying, "I have anxiously waited all my life for this. Nothing else matters to me right now, sweet Emma." I closed my eyes and pretended I was dreaming. This throbbing pain tore through me. When I opened my eyes, he was still inside me. He looked down and smiled. He said, "This pussy is a miracle. I can't believe that I was able to get half of my big dick inside my precious coochie tonight.

"I have been with two adult women and they could not handle Ole Bo's long dick. Every woman I have been with says my dick is too big. This is perfect, Mrs. Brown. I am so proud of you. All that prepping has paid off. Our preparations have expanded this young pussy so big Ole Bo can just glide in there right now.

"Do you feel my baby moving and grinding deep inside of that pussy? I am all the way up around your womb. It is up there where my baby is. I have given him plenty of honey today and into the night. I love how it feels! You are so good, and this pussy is scorching. I love it." He looked down and said, "Ole Bo hears you hollering and moaning. I can feel you. I like your wiggling. Are you trying to throw it to big daddy? You are stroking this long big dick, young gal. The last twenty minutes I tested you. Mrs. Brown you have not missed a stroke. Yes, young mama, you have thrown that pussy around big Bo's dick. You were stroking just like Clarence Carter sings his song 'I Am Stroking.' You are stroking to the east, you are stroking to the west, and you are stroking to the one you love the best, Ole Bo Brown. This feeling is worth a million dollars . . . It is unreal, Ole Bo's got most of your new dick inside of you. Oh, oh, it is so hot and good. I can't stop. Here is, here is, Mrs. Emma Brown, I am giving you every drop of come I got. This is an express load of hot come from Ole Bo to his new bride. This is a special delivery to his growing baby. You just gave me all of you this is perfect. I have dreamed of this since you were eight years old. Your body developed so fast you look like you were twelve years old when you were just eight years old. I have never seen a girl as enticing as you. You would switch pass me I would get a hard just watching you walk. Mrs. Emma, you had no idea how your little ass was swinging in the wind. You were born sexy. It is no secret that the old men on this block got a hard on watching you walk. I dreamed many times how it would feel. Reality is here. You made my wildest fantasy come true. It feels like Ole Bo is in another world. Many nights I imaged of how it would feel to be inside of you. Now Bo dick knows. This is superb. Today the Judge gave Jake Brown his official permission. I am authorized to ride all the way up inside this sweet hot coochie. I don't have to imagine anymore. Sweet Emma, this hole between your thighs is my treasure sachet. Ole Bo has been patiently treasure hunting for two years. On this wedding day, big Bo just opened up my treasure with this big dick of yours. Even after two years of training, I had to struggle to get half of my long dick in that tight pussy. You see, Mrs. Emma, I can call it my own personal coochie or pussy.

He looked at my stomach smiling. "Your husband loves the thrill I feel as I touched these precious diamonds. Ole Jake just had to get to the bottom of your hot box . . . I felt the magic when I did. Yes, indeed. I tore the rest of that hymen I left in you when I touch my black diamond. That was the balance of my trophy. You got my black hot diamond deep in that sizzling hole. Big Bo is very greedy." He slapped my butt and started rocking. He said, "I must get to my crown jewel at the stroke of midnight. What a wonderful wedding present. We have been making love over twelve hours. We stared at ten thirty yesterday morning. We have fucked into a new day." Finally, I started pleading again. "Please Mr. Brown. Can we stop and let me rest, dear husband, just for a little while? You are killing me. It feels like you are tearing me up down there. You said you were my friend. Friends don't hurt friends." "I am not your friend no more," he snapped. "I am your husband." His body was wet with sweat as he held me down. He climbed off me and lay down beside. He put his heavy hairy leg across my legs. "Okay, let us talk about it."

Mr. Brown said, "This little hairy thing between your legs is mine forever." I lay there moaning and crying. I thought maybe if I acted a different way he will think I am cooperating with him. I stopped crying. I reached over and kissed him. He smiled. He said, "Oh, my wife just kissed me for the first time." I said, "Yes, Mr. Brown, you know how to thrill me." He asked can you say the word. I asked what word. He said can you say I like the way I fuck you. I sniffled and said Yes Mr. Brown my coochie feels so good when you are fucking me. He jumped up and danced around he said that's my woman. Talk that talk to me baby. Ole Bo is going to keep you happy. I am going to make you feel so good you will be begging for more of your dick." My rapist started grinning from ear to ear. He said, "I know how to make it good to you my dear sweetheart. You didn't hear yourself moaning and begging for more. I heard your pleading, saying stop, I know that trick. That means Give me more, big Bo and I gave you more. A few more round and I am going to rest. You will wear your husband out the first day." I said, "No. No. I don't want any more." Jake said, "You don't have to be embarrassed about it. You can have this dick anytime you want it." I just laid there and cried. He said, "You can stop begging, Mrs. Emma. I can't believe you are crying for more." He kept saying I would get used to it. Now he will never let me get away from him.

This ole man did not care about my tenderness. He reached over and kissed me on my mouth. He whispered it is supposed to hurt my little precious Emma. That sound of a woman begging and crying turns a man on. This makes him know he is doing a good job of fucking. Those grunts you were making let me know I was stroking deep inside my new coochie. He carried me to the bath room. There were many packages of disposal douches beside the commode. Mr. Brown asked do you know how to use a douche? I said no sir. He said lay back in the tube. Read the directions big girl. Place the douche up inside my pussy and wash it out. Matter of fact you need to use two douches. I shot so much come up in you one will not cleanse you. My sweet baby you are loaded with my milk of life. I call that my love juice. Once you finish with the douche sat in the tub of warm water and soak. He let me soak for a long while. Later he showered me and carried me back to the chair. Smiling he said I had to change those sheets we have soaked them with our love juice. Emma, I think if I thrill my new pussy a few more times I can hit the jack pot again. I am determined to get at least three-fourths of your hungry dick in my soft hot pussy again. We know that was not a one-time thing. Mr. Brown placed me in the middle of his bed smiling. He climbed up on top of me again. This big man forced his penis inside of me. It felt like someone had punched me in the bottom of my stomach. He rocked as he rode me. I can't count how many times he sprayed his thick juice inside of me. He whispered you are all woman. His salty Sweat was running down in my face. The sweat dripped from his body all over me. Finally, he got up off of me. He let me rest. He said drink a little wine this can't hurt my baby. I checked with the doctor. He said, "It is okay as long as you just relax." He said, "You could have a small glass once a day. Mrs. Emma, I know you can tolerate it. Hell you had a drink of wine every day the last year or so. Remember I just told you I soaked your candy in wine every day. When you got older I changed to gin. Drink, my princess."

Mr. Brown placed me back in the chair. "Here we go, my sweet rose." Mr. Brown thrilled me over and over again. I lost count of the times he gave me tantalizing orgasm. I hate Mr. Jake Brown, but I like the way he thrilled my body. I was trembling. He looked up and said, "I love those sounds you made when I thrill that pussy in this chair. It is even better when I am inside of this pussy and you are wiggling that ass. You stroke like a professional. Oh yes, Mrs. Emma, I have been with a prostitute. She was not as good as you. Look at you miss bashful lover. Oh, Mrs. Emma, you are so greedy. I know you want more. Big Bo heard you pleading and begging for more. This coochie wants more. This is wonderful I have done a good job making this hot coochie good to you big mommy. Quickly he carried me to the bed. Jake rode me as he filled me up with his warm juice. He said I ain't worked up a sweat like this in all my life. No mam not working in the plant or in the cotton field ever got me this hot. Our bodies are on fire baby. Yes, mam, we are burning up this bed. Oh yeah, this is a well-deserved sweat. I saved it just for you little mommy. You are better than any of those adult women I have been with.

"That right little Emma you just became a woman and some kind of woman you are. I will kill a man if I ever think another man touch this. This is one thing a man wont share. I am just breaking you in on our honeymoon."

My mind went back to Jake playing horsey with me on grandma front porch. When I complained about the way the stick felt in his pocket. He said something about breaking me in for my new saddle. This ole goat played up to me like he was trying to protect me. Today, he was taking what he had sat his mind a long time ago. He was a sly ole fox with his mind sat on taking all of my young innocent body. God help me is all I can say now.

Lord God the preacher didn't teach us about this at church. None of the women at church said anything except don't be so fast. I didn't know what that meant. The teacher at school didn't tell us this would happen. They showed us a video about our period. That is all we were told. Getting married is for grown people not a child like me. Why didn't someone tell me how a man would treat a helpless kid? I believed Jake would protect me. He said he would never let anybody hurt me. Now he is tearing my body apart. This pain is worse than anything I know. His big rod is making my whole body throb. This big man rod fells like a hose filling me up with his hot juice. This is the most horrible pain I ever experience in my life . . .

I never have been alone with a man without my grandma. Why didn't she tell me what would happen to me when I came to Mr. Brown's house? Now she is not here to help me. No one told me that a man would pin me down in a bed, molest and rape a child. I am just a youngster. I have only been in the bed with my Granny. I don't understand why this old goat is taking advantage of me like this. I did not ask for this. I don't like it at all. I am sad and he doesn't care. My plan was to wait and have sex when I finish college. This mean man doesn't care about anybody but his self. He seemed to enjoy bringing pain to my tiny body. Helpless, I lay and cry as he used my body as a tool, but nobody cares. I feel like a cast away on a lonely island. This makes me know I am totally alone in this miserable life. I am trapped here in an ole man's fantasy. There is no hope for me. My life will never be the same.

The sad part of this nightmare is I don't know how I got here. Neither my Granny nor my Poppy saw this coming, or did they? I surely didn't. I am miserable and horrified. He is very glad. Laying on me huffing like a big hog. He sounds like granddaddy's big hog in the pen. His hands are all over me. I read about beautiful romance in literature books and magazines. It was my dream to graduate from college. Then a professional man could romanced and cherish me. I planned to have a young lover that would marry me and we would have a great life together. What a disaster this is. What can a twelve-year-old girl do with this old man? We were told in school that you could not get married until you were eighteen years old. That is the law my social studies teacher taught us in class. Well I am not eighteen. Today I am married at age twelve years old right here in Alabama.

This is a new day I stop trying to resist Jake. He is too tall and heavy. He was so strong I could not move. I felt powerless. This evil man rode me like the cowboy ride their horse in the movies. Now I understand what he was talking about riding a filly as he rides me like a young mare. I hate the sound of him yelling, "Get up, girl."

"Just look at ole Bo riding his young hot filly." He slapped my butt and yelled, "I love it. I just lassoed me a young wild filly." He looked down on me and said, "Look up there on the wall. See that hat rack, Mrs. Emma, that big black cowboy hat hanging on the wall is mine. I bought my black cowboy hat especially for our ride. I am enjoying my ride so much I can't stop to put on my cowboy hat on I brought for our honeymoon. It a day late I was so excited yesterday I didn't get a chance to put on my hat. Cowboy must have his hat on when he rides his filly. I was so excited I missed that part of our ceremony. Ole Bo needed his cowboy hat yesterday for those sweet rides I had . . ." Finally, he got tired and stopped for a while. He laid a towel over my legs. I was still aching and cramping. He yelled buckle up young gal. It scared me even more. He looked at me and yelled Ole Bo is in control. I told you I was getting you use to riding in your new saddle. Actual Mrs. Brown you are my filly I am riding inside my saddle. I tried to get up and he said oh no I will tell you when to get up. I am not through with you yet big gal . . . He threw his big leg across my body again. He fell off to sleep. I tried to wiggle from under him. All my sliding didn't work I could not go anywhere.

This night mare started about eleven in the morning. The sun is bright outside. Six hours later I am locked in a house with my rapist. I want to go home to Granny. Jake went over and poured some rum in a glass. He drank the first glass. He kisses me and said, "You can't have this." He said, "Here is a little rum for you. Drank it now I don't have a lot of time to waste, big filly. I am ready to mount up again. This rum will help you handle the rest of our honeymoon a little bit better. I know this is a whole lot of man to handle. I am so glad I stretched your young hot body so I could get in it."

Jake walked over and took his cowboy hat off. "Baby, your fire is too hot I can't wear this hat while I ride you." He said, "Okay, Ole Bo is ready to ride into the last home stretch he climbed on top of me and yelled git up big gal. My hot filly is ready to ride again." He slapped my butt harder and harder as he rammed his big rod hard inside of my vagina passed my cervix and into my stomach.

I stopped counting the time his fire hose sprayed inside my body. I guess my little body couldn't hold all his warm juice he was squirting out. Maybe, this is what the science teacher meant by ejaculation. It was a big word I didn't really pay any attention then, but now the big word says what he is doing to me. Right now Jake is ejaculating inside me. That's right it is happening to me a helpless motherless child. There is nothing about this night I want to remember.

I was so weak when he finally finished. The next morning, he said, "Look out the window, Mrs. Brown. This is another life lesson. You see my car. I own that, baby. I can ride in it when I want to. I can drive it fast or slow or slow and fast. I can turn it however I want to. I can drive backward or forward. That is what our marriage license says. I can do to you and with you. I can ride it as long as I want to. It's mine. You are mine now just like that car I going to ride you when I want as long as I want to and there is nothing you can do about it I am your husband."

Jake was smiling as he turned over and climbed up on me again. "Hee-haw Ole Bo is a Wild West cowboy just riding his young hot filly on third full day of our honey moon. I am making plenty of honey this weekend. My bed can't hold all this honey. I am loaded for this little hot filly. I went by the drug store and got me some red rooster pill. I told the drug store man I had a hot young gal and I need to be able to get hard without any trouble. So far I have only needed them once. Oh yes, I am back in the saddle again." He laughed and said, "You got a good one, baby." This big man was smiling from ear to ear as he coved my young innocent body. These painful rides tore my little vagina even more. He paid me no attention as I laid there grunting. He would finish and roll off of me. His stops last for a little while. I tried to get up; he would not let me get up. Helpless, I lay in Jake's puddle of sticky juice. His juicy pond got bigger and bigger after he spayed up inside of me and the juice overflowed. I prayed and hoped this was the last time. Not so fast he grinned. He would start again huffing, puffing, and yelling my name. "Oh yes, Miss Emma, you are all mine." The pain is indescribable I like to read and learn a lot of big words. I never learn the word Jake is calling my body parts. He is calling my private parts names I never heard before. These days have been a nightmare I never want to remember. It lasted Thursday, Friday, Saturday and Sunday. It felt like someone was mutilating me over and over again.

Time stood still I was not able to get out of bed without help for one month. Whenever Mr. Brown was riding me, he said he was fucking me. This is a new word for me. He worked cooks, fed, and fucked me. Not one day has passed that Jake did not ride me. His big tool is too long and too big to fit all of it inside of me. He said. "Oh, well." He said I made it fit. He smiled and said, "I have designed this coochie to fit me." All of his body pounding against me has wounded me so badly. How can this be good? When he was finished, he smiled and said, "Women are born to satisfy a man. She got to give him whatever he wants, whenever he wants it, and however he wants to get it. Get used to it and soon you will like it, baby."

During this first month of marriage, the daily encounters had left my body in agonizing pain. He gives me two pain pills he had from an old back injury he received at work. I was too sore and weak to walk. He locked both doors when he went to work. Jake smile when I finally got up. I was grunting, sitting on the side of the bed.

I told him it hurt to walk. He picked me up and took me to the bathroom. Grinning he said, "Oh yea, I am just introducing you to the real life of a married woman. You are so blessed. I molded you. I did a good job of prepping you to protect you. Listen, young tender thang, about fifteen years ago, I was engaged to a nice woman. Something happen to this fine young woman. I didn't prep her. I deeply regret that I tore up my fiancée female organs. The injury was so bad she had to have surgery. We dated for a while longer. She stayed sick. Finally she developed cervical cancer and died. I learn from that experience.

"When you were eight years old, I decided I was going to have you as my wife. I started to work on your body. Thankfully, those exercises I gave you stretched you. The more your body got use to the stretching riding your horsey the more relaxes you became. This made it better for us. This is the reason I started training your little tender body years ago. I made sure not to make that same mistake again I made with my fiancée'. You are too special to me for me to hurt my big gal. After a while you will be begging me for more. Just wait and see.

"Oh, how I love playing inside the fuzzy stronghold. Gradually, I got your body trained to loosen up. You became comfortable to the touch of my staff. That's right I got you use to my staff. Oh, Mrs. Emma, I must get you used to these new words. See I name my hand my staff. Yes sir, I went to the promise land right in front of Granny. All that practicing prepared your young body for this honeymoon. I am glad this entrance wasn't so hard on you. It took twenty-four months of horsey rides to get you ready for this week end as we celebrate our wedding. I am taking it easy with you little girl even now.

"If I had not stretched your body our honeymoon could be a disaster. Yes sir, I was training you with just part of my rod and staff. Many evenings I played inside this pussy until it got nice and wet. When you were riding the horsey, you were sitting straddled my dick. Every horsey ride, I jarred your little tight hole open a little more each time. A year later, it all paid off. I was in. Once I got inside without hurting you, I had completed my task. I know I had it made. The more I played inside of this pussy the greedier I got. I hated when Saturday and Sunday came. That meant a day without playing in this coochie. Remember I only came around five days a week to see you and Mrs. Mattie. That was such a thrill when I was able to get my big hand inside of you. Playing inside of the hot box sent me home with wet pants every day. That is the reason I brought my workbag with me. It coved my wet pants every evening. It made me so hard as I played inside of you. I jacked off on myself five days a week. I made it so good to you, my precious rose. You would relax riding your horsey your legs would dangle in the air. I loved seeing the smile on your face as you relaxed and dropped off to sleep. You were so relaxed your body would go limb. Ole Bo enjoyed playing inside this pussy. Your expression said you love it as much I did it without attracting your grandma attention. Matter of fact you and Granny was smiling as I glided into your precious castle in plain sight

"I am a natural born lover Mrs. Brown, I am sorry I can't help but brag. That was unforgettable. Can you not say with all honesty that you didn't like your daily rides. I gave you many, many good horsey rides the last couple of years. Didn't you enjoy them as much as I did?"

I was embarrassed. I looked down and said, "Yes, I enjoyed my horsey rides."

"You said they were good rides, Emma. I know you enjoyed your thrills." I felt shame as I admitted I enjoyed my horsey rides. I did not know what he was doing. I thought it was all fun.

"Man I never will forget those big smiles on your face as you rode your horsey, big girl. You wanted it. I know you did. Your grandmother was happy to see the smile I put on your face. Look at your big banana. I will teach you how to suck it later. This big tall man stood up with his huge rod in his hand."

The sight of this weapon made me faint again. When I woke up he was fanning me. There was a cold rag on my forehead. My screams spread throughout the house. "My god," I cried, "that big long piece of black pipe is too big for a cow. It should be against the law for a man to stick that in a child. I am going to the police and tell them what you have done to me. How can this be right? If you tore up an adult woman, what will happen to me. You raped me! Mr. Brown, you have kept me against my will and molested me over and over. You should go to jail. This is against the law for a man to show that big rod to a child." I kept screaming I want to go home. "Please, Mr. Brown, please carries me back home to my granny. I would not tell anybody what you have done to me."

He put on his underwear. Smiling, he said, "Okay, little girl, this might be too much for you right now." He grabbed me up and said, "You are not going anywhere. You better not tell anyone. If you do something will happen to your granny. I promise you that. The police cannot do anything about what a man does with his wife. I have this piece of paper that says it is legal for me to do what I am doing. I am your husband. This marriage certificate says I can do whatever I want with your fine little hot body. Remember, Mrs. Brown, legally a woman cannot testify against her husband little young blood. The law is on the husband's side."

Jake went into the kitchen and cooked a meal. He picked me up and carried me to the table. "I love you, Mrs. Emma Brown. Don't let me hear you use the word rape again. That could get us in trouble. If I go to jail, who will take care of you and my baby? We are in this together. Listen, baby, I will be easy with you. It is going to take time and patience. I truly believed that all those long hours of stretching you would make this much easier. I thought you would be able to handle it better than you have. You are still tender and young. I believe in time your body will finish stretching to fit your fishing rod. Yes sir, I went fishing as I gave you your ride. I fondly remembered those good ole rough rides. The long rides gave you enough lubrication that I could ride Jake Junior right up in you. I just have to glorify those great thrills. You must learn to trust me like Granny did. Listen this is how much your granny trusted me I know you are sick of me talking about our courtship. Yes believe it or not that was our courtship.

"About a year ago, your granny asked me to pick up a package. I said I will be glad to pick up your package. She said, 'Oh yes, please tell the clerk to send me six pairs of panties size 8 for this growing great-granddaughter of mine.' That was a big break for me. My, oh my, I loved that privilege she gave me. It was my big break. Mrs. Mattie did not know what an opportunity that presented to me. Later when I came from the store, Mrs. Mattie smiled, saying, 'That little gal has grown out of all of her under wears.' Smiling, I said, 'Yes, Mrs. Mattie, she is spreading out.' I carefully picked your panties. I selected those pretty panties with no elastic in the leg. Those open-bottom panties help me reach my goal. I had a plan in mind from that time forward. I am sorry you were deceived. A man has got to do to get what he wants. You would never agree to have sex with me if I had asked. Hell, you didn't know nothing about being with a man. That was the farthest thing from your childish innocent girl mind. There are not a lot of pure girl in this town. Mrs. Emma, I heard the many men around town talking about you being so pure. I just couldn't wait to make you mine. That is the real reason I had to steal it. The mere fact I was sitting so close to a pure girl made me very horney. It would have killed me if someone else had taken your innocence before I did . . . I beat them all to the prize. I am not sorry. I will be lying if I said I did." He picked me up and took me to the bathroom. Jake bathed me and dried me off. He kissed me and carried me into the living room. "Mrs. Emma Brown, I need your two cents to settle down and deal with reality. You are not going anywhere. You are not going to tell any anyone about us.

"It is too late. I am the only help you will get. Your grandparents will not pay for nor take care of my wife and baby. I will let you rest for a while. I am going into the kitchen and make you're an eggnog milk shake. Yes mama my daddy taught me that those fresh raw eggs will help you. That will be good for both of you. Let me make this plain you can't go anywhere. You are now my property.

"I promise I will not attempt stretching you too fast. I hope I have not torn your tender organs down there. I tried not to give you more than you can stand. Ole Jake has to take care of his new family. I got a bonus. I got a spouse and baby at the same time.

"Just look at you now. I must take you shopping to buy the Browns more clothes. These clothes are too small. We must get maternity clothes for the two of you. The doctor said you are four months pregnant when we married. We have been together a month and the size 16 clothes are too small.

"This was the best way to make sure you were mine. I take great pride in my accomplishments with you. My baby is making your stomach expand. Your whole little bottom is spreading. Do you understand Baby girl. I started to cry again. When you deliver my baby it will leave you big and open. I will make sure to tell the doctor I don't want your bottom stitched up too small. I will explain to the doctor we need his help. I know he will understand. Then I can follow the baby's birth and it won't hurt you. Your body will be reshaped to fit your stallion. I am going to have a rocking good time. Until then I will follow the opening my baby makes for ole Bo. Your body will change each month making room for your baby and your husband. I know the baby is a boy

"Once you open up to deliver Jake junior I will complete your training. You will have stretch enough to birth my child. That big opening will allow me to follow without doing any further damage. Four months from now everything will be just right. This will make it easy for your body to adjust to your husband's full size rod."

I looked up at him and begged, "Will you please take me to the doctor."

"Hell no, they might try to say I hurt you. I know the law. I paid the clerk to take care of my business. You are not going to start any trouble for me. I will go by the drug store and get something. Ole Jake got to be careful. Your age says you are still a little young child, but you have a woman's body. Just look at your breasts and butt. You are not thirteen years old yet, Mrs. Emma, but you have the body of a grown woman. We will have to wait until next year for you to turn thirteen. I will never know what the doctor or the hospital might try to do to get me in trouble like they did your granddaddy.

I stayed in bed those four weeks as Jake raped me over and over. He gladly celebrated his trophy every night. When the pond of his manhood soaked the bed, he would bathe me and change the linen. He fixed food for us. We ate and watched television. The weekends, Jake is off from work. He spends his weekend inside of me. I am so glad to see Monday morning come.

Early Monday morning, my rapist was grinning as he got ready for work. Jake turned the bills of his cap backward before he goes off to work. He always says, "When the boys look at my cap they all will know what I have been doing on the weekend. I have just done the man thing. Yea, I brag every week about my trophy." He said it took a long time to make this announcement to the boys.

When he came home from work he continued to talk about his past. He said the boys used to measure to see who had the biggest rod. "I won every time." He sniggled. "Some of these old women around here in the community and in the church told me they would not let me tear them open with this rod. Some of them would not even talk to me because of big Bo's reputation around town. The real truth is these old women wanted me to fuck them. No thanks, I wanted this young girl. I got this pussy for myself. Oh well, they miss out on a good damn ride. Now it all belongs to you, Mrs. Brown, every inch of it.

"Emma, have you ever watch a cowboy movie quietly?" I said yes. He said, "Okay, I am doing just what the cowboy does to a filly. The rule says I am your cowboy. I must tame you, my young filly. That's what I am doing right now to you. I have lassoed you.

"Now I must continue to break your spunk, which means breaking your resistance. After I train you with my hands and my rod, you will obey. You will jump when I say jump. You will lay down when I say lay. You will open up without a struggle. Whatever position I put you in, you must stay in that position until I finish. Do you understand what I am saying? You will not get up or get tired until I say so.

"You will suck what I tell you as long as I say so. I got a hard banana when I say suck, you will smile and say, 'Yes, big daddy.' You will suck as long as I want you to. That is just what I mean. I will train you on that later. Believe me, my young wife, I am breaking you a little at a time you couldn't stand it all in twelve months. Your little young body got to get use to your new master's rod and staff. I am your new cowboy and only rider. You got that, my baby girl."

Tearfully, I said, "Yes, sir."

"Every part of your body belongs to me. I am your boss just like ole boss is my master at work I am your master at home and everywhere you go, every day of the week 24/7. I am in charge of my Emma. When you lived at home, Mule was your boss. You will get used to it. You are going to love being my little filly. You just wait and see."

I nodded my head. "Yes, sir."

"You can forget that sir mess."

This new life of mine is so sad. Now I remember the many stories about slaves. Back in the day, the young girl had not control of their body. She had to do what every ole master told her to do or her family would pay the price. This is 1951. I feel like slavery is still here. My mind drifted off. I heard Jake talking, but I don't really want to hear what he had to say. He represented the ole slave master in my life. Jake reached over and rubbed my stomach. He was smiling from ear to ear. "Yea, I got something to help your granny to nod off while I prep you. This old fox got you pregnant right there in front of your grandmother . . . I say that's slick. Don't you agree? Jake, the sly old fox is enjoying my victory." His face lights up when he sucked my breast. That silly grin is on his face every time as he say, "Poor baby, I meant to get a little bit on the sly, not get you pregnant. That was an accident, but it all good. I am not sorry about nothing that happened.

"I gave you a belly full, yes sir, right in the wide open outdoors. Many of the old folk in the community passed by smiling and waving hello to the three of us sitting on the front porch. Some asked how are things doing over there? I always smiled and said we are doing good and fine, thanks. Sometime I would say life couldn't be any better. There was a smile on my face as I worked my magic. I enjoyed every minute. No one every suspected anything wrong was going on. I fooled one and all. You never suspected what was happening to you, my young naive girl. I made sure Grandma rest while I prepared this young tender body. My treats made sure she nodded off. I knew what I was doing. Oh yea, I puncture it, and you didn't even know what was happening to you. I am sorry to keep going over the same thing, but it makes me feel so good just to know I got away with it.

"Just remember the rule when I am inside you. I am feeding my baby. That's what the ole men taught me. Some folk say it good for the baby. You know I am going to stay up in you as much as possible to feed my baby. Ha-ha I don't have to worry about these little class-mate boys wanting you anymore.

"Bless your little immature heart. No no, Ole Bo got blessed. Just look at me now. I could not dream this up. I knows you are good. That ole granny of yours made sure she kept all the young bucks away from you.

"Grandma Mattie even kept you away from Ole drunk Mule. I came around every day to keep Mule in his place. He never tried to bother you either, did he?" I looked away in horror. He said, "You would tell me if he did, would you?" I sniffled and said, "Jake, I don't live with Poppy anymore." His voice changed. "I would not stand for what he did to Bessie. Believe me I would have killed him if he did. I was going to make sure that nothing did happening to you.

"He is a good man, but I know he takes sex from any female around when he is drunk. He like them young too, just like me. Therefore, since we both like the same thing, I felt I had to protect you from him. That old drunk great-granddaddy was not going to rape you like he did his own daughter. I was going to make sure I was the first and only. Thanks to Mrs. Mattie, I am a happy man. I saved up a nice little nest egg for her that's why she is happy. She can't let Mule know how much. He will kill her or maybe he won't. If she gives him his money he will be alright. He won't have to feed and clothe you anymore.

"I know she has protected you from the young boys. Yes, she did she kept you pure. She kept young Emma virginity well protected. Ha-ha all that security was just for her Jake. I kept my true feelings to myself. She never knew my intention. Mrs. Mattie said she felt like I was her son. Maybe she loves me. Now I am officially in the family. Ha-ha, the poor old woman didn't know she was protecting my interest. We sang and told jokes. It was good for her too. I made the day for that pitiful old lady. Nobody else would go around her because of Mule. She needed my company, and I needed to be near you. I knew what I was doing. All of those treats I brought for her paid off. They gave me an additional benefits.

"She watched over my cherry. I know you are a virgin. I will give you anything in this world. I am the happiest man in the world right now . . . Oh yes, I am sitting on top of the world right now. I couldn't ask for anything better.

"I got my own young virgin. She is pure, tight, and tender. This big rod of mine has marked you. I am not worried. None of these little boys can fit you when I get thru with you. Years ago, I learn when I finished with one of my woman she was so big no other man could fit her. So little girl you are mine and mine alone. No man will be able to enjoy you when I get through with you.

"I call that Bo's mark. Ha-ha, Ole Bo knows what to do. You were eight years old when I set my eyes on this. On your eight birthday, I said, 'She is mine. I have waited four years for this cherry.' My plan was to wait until you were at least thirteen. Well, Ole Bo got greedy and I got you at the wonderful age of twelve. Here we are. It

is so good, Mrs. Emma. That right, you are now Mrs. Jake Brown."
I kept grunting.

"I am sorry, baby. Let's try to get you up out of the bed." He sat
me up. "Okay, let walk to the bathroom." My body was trembling in
pain. I yelled, "I cannot do it. Grandma came by today. She tried to
get me up. I was in so much pain. She brought the chamber to me.
She said to tell you to take me to the doctor when you get home. I
didn't have my insurance card so she could not carry me herself. Help
me please."

Jake dressed me. He drove me to the hospital. Jake said, "Let's
practice your answers. When the nurse asks you date of birth, you
will use your sister's birthday. She is eighteen years old. Make sure to
tell them you are married. That will stop any suspense." Moaning, I
said, "Yes, sir." He yelled, "Don't say, 'Yes, sir,' to me in the hospital."

When we arrived at the emergency room, the nurse saw how
much pain I was in she took me back to a room. My temp was 102.
My blood pressure was 210/102. The doctor came in and examined me. He asked how many months was my pregnancy. I said five
months. He shook his head. He said, "I am admitting you now." The
doctor told the nurse, "Call up stairs to OB and tell the nurse I am
sending this patient up to them immediately." The doctor looked at
Jake and said, "I need you to step outside a few minutes, sir. I must
check her at once."

Jake said, "I am her husband. I want to see what is going on."

The doctor insisted, "No, sir, you must leave the room now, or
I will call security. Jake stomped out of the room, mad. The nurse
assisted the doctor as he carefully examined me. This doctor was very
kind. He looked at me and asked, "What happen to you?"

I said, "What do you mean, Doctor?"

"Have you had a lot of pain?" I was scared. Softly I said, "Yes,
sir, I have been hurting for the last month."

"We are running test on the blood the nurse sent to the lab. We
will let you know what we find out." Nurses were putting in an IV,
another was taking more blood. One nurse put two oxygen tubes in
my nose. Everything was moving so fast. The doctor gave me med-

icine for pain. I went to sleep. When I woke up, I was on the OB floor. Time just slipped away.

A group of doctors came to my bedside. The older doctor said, "Your blood pressure is too high to carry you to surgery now. I see the admitting doctor was concerned about your internal injuries. We looked at the x-rays and see your female organs are ripped and torn badly. Your ovaries are swollen and infected. I must get you stabilized first. Next I must get a gynecologist to repair your rips, and then we can put a net in to hold this baby in. If we don't do something now, you will deliver in the next few hours. Whatever infection we are dealing with will be treated appropriately.

I slept a lot. The next day, my doctor came in smiling. He said, "I see you are awake, young lady. You gave us all a scare. Where is your husband?" Jake stepped in the door. The doctor said, "We are taking her to surgery tomorrow. First we have to repair the damages threatening this baby. We will put a cerclage inside her to keep the baby safe until her delivery time." The doctor walked up to Jake and said, "According to my training, when I checked inside this young-ster, I found a very immature and underdeveloped body. There are numerous internal injuries. I don't know how she has handled the pain. One thing for sure, she did not do this damage to herself." The doctor asked my granny to step out a minute.

"I am obligated to protect my patient. Outside, Emma has the height, big breast, and buttock, her body has developed beyond her years. Inside where it counts, Mrs. Brown doesn't have the body of an eighteen-year-old woman. She is your wife. I will let it go. It is my obligation to do what is best for my patient. Thus, I checked the damage organs. She could not bruise the organs along. Someone injured her internally. That leaves only you. I believe your genital is very large. It has damage these undeveloped organs inside this young body. This is the third patient that came into this hospital with inju-ries from you, Jake Brown. Mr. Brown, you have ripped and torn this young female body extensively. We are going to do what we can to save her. This is a very serious case. The baby is at risk now. When this is over and she goes home, you can't have sex with her until the baby arrived. After the baby's delivery, you must wait four months, Mr. Brown, before you can have sex with her. Do you understand?"

Jake nodded. "Yes, sir." Jake turned to me and smiled and said, "I am sorry, baby. I hurt you. He turned to the doctor and said, "I never meant to hurt her. She is so hot, Doctor. I will try to control myself when I get her home." The doctor did not smile. He said, "If this was not your wife, I would file a sexual assault and rape charge on you." The doctor left my room. Jake bent over to me and said, "That doctor can't tell me what to do with my wife." Six days later, I was better. I was up walking in my room. The surgeon came in and said he was able to repair all the rips and tears to my female organs. This doctor ordered antibiotics and other meds to help me get well. I feel so much better. I was smiling when Granny came to see me. I told her I wanted to go home with her. Granny dropped her head and said, "Baby, I would love to take you home with me. In my heart, I know you would not be safe at my house with Mule now. He was grumbling just the other day. Mule said, 'Jake got a good gal. Hell, I didn't finish my inspection,' he grumbled. 'I had not fully declared her value or set my dowry before she was gone.'" I kissed Granny and said, "I am sorry. I hope I didn't get you into any trouble." She smiled and said, "Jake sure wanted you he gave Mule double the asking."

The doctor discharged me. He told Jake, "I mean for her body to rest. There is to be no sex for the next six months. Before the surgery, I said sex after four months. After careful examination, she must have extra time to heal before you have sex with her. Are we clear, Mr. Brown?"

Jake nodded. "Yes, sir. It is going to be very hard for me."

Dr. Jackson said, "I have a health care team that will come into the home and check on Emma. A nurse will come to see her. The nurse assistance will come weekly for four weeks. Our social workers will check on her living environment. Regardless of what you say as her husband, we are obligated to check on her safety. It seems like she is afraid of you. Is there a reason for such fear, Mr. Brown?"

Jake said, "No, sir, I would never hurt Emma. I love her. I just got carried away having a young virgin as my wife. There was never a time I set out to hurt her. I am a little older than my wife, so I was trying to make her happy. It was my goals to thrill her not tear her." The doctor did not smile. He said, "My team is very concerned about this problem." Dr. Jackson left the room. There was silence in my room. Jake looked scared. "When are they going to discharge you, Mrs. Brown? I don't feel comfortable here. These doctors could try to get me in trouble."

Three days later, I began to feel better. There was someone holding my hand. I look up. It was my great-grandma. She hugged me and said, "You are blessed to be alive the doctor said. Jake is more worried about that baby than he is about you. Get better, baby. I will be back tomorrow. I have been here every day since you have been in this hospital."

The next day, the doctor said, "I am your obstetrician/gynecologist. You are so young. I am going to explain what we found. I have Janet my RN here for you. She will answer any question you might think of later. The blood tests reveal you have two different kind of infection chlamydia and gonorrhea. These are bacteria disease. Neustria Gonnacoysis is the bacteria that cause gonorrhea. If it is transmitted to your baby, it could have some adverse effect. The other sexually transmitted disease is caused by chlamydia trachoma's bacteria. Have you ever been taught about sexually transmitted diseases?"

I said, "My teacher gave us a handout on it, but I don't understand all these big words. I want to answer you honestly, sir."

"Okay, let me ask you this, what other man have you had sex with?"

I sat up and said, "Only Mr. Brown." The doctor said, "Hum, I am familiar with Mr. Jake Brown. We will talk later. When your husband comes in, tell him to come to the desk and ask for Janet or Dorothy. They are my two nurses. We must talk to him as soon as possible. We took samples from several places in you. We found gonorrhea present in your cervix, vagina, and urethra. It is possible to be present in your rear end. We have not checked your rectum, but it could very well be there. We are glad it not syphilis. The risk increased with a pregnant woman. I am glad we found chlamydia midway. You are going into your sixth month. There are some risks. Our immediate treatment will help avoid miscarriage, premature birth, or still birth. I am starting two new IV medicines today."

That night when Jake came in, I asked him, "Why did you give me gonorrhea and chlamydia? Now, Mr. Brown, my body is full of sexually transmitted diseases that you gave me. You have bruised and torn me up inside. I hope you are proud now, Mr. Jake Brown. You have wrecked my life."

"Mrs. Emma Brown, I thought I was cured. I did have some incidents a few years ago. I was treated by my doctor. He said I would be fine. It is good we got you here to the hospital in time. I would not want anything to happen to my baby. The doctors will make you well soon. This modern medicine can take care of these things. There is nothing to worry about. You will be fine." Tears washed my face. I asked, "How you could do this to me?"

Mr. Brown dropped his head, saying, "I didn't know I was ripping and tearing you when you were moaning and groaning? I thought those sounds you were making said Ole Bo was making you feel good as I thrilled you. You made sounds of joy when I gave you oral sex. Later when I overpowered you and took what I wanted, I felt proud. I thought the sounds meant it felt good to you.

"The old men in my life taught me once you overpower the female, eventually she will enjoy the sexual experience. My daddy said a woman may resists at first, but she will love it after a few struggles. The elder men in my family taught me never to pay the female's begging any attention during the struggle. These same men said just tuned her noise out when you are going for the prize. My dad was in this conversation. He said later on, 'Son, this same woman will be looking for you. She will want you to keep giving her more sex. She will be under your power.' They told me I could get great thrills again and again as you teach the female who is the master of your pussy. Because of these teaching, I really enjoyed my conquest over you. Emma, this rough sex with you made me feel so macho. When I won the struggle, it affirmed to me I had certified your pussy as my exclusive property.

"This is an old-fashion rule that has been handed down through many generations. This sexual conquest is a big thrill for a man. I paraded around among the guys at work like a rooster in the barn yard. Bragging to the men on my job how I had taken control of this young hot body of yours. I grew up believing the everlasting special thrill came when you restrained a female and take sex from her over a prolong time, not just once, it affirm your manhood. That is why I couldn't let you up. The sounds of struggle really turn me on. I was trained that way. Now that you are here in the hospital, this is a whole different ball game. The doctors are in charge. I remember your voice saying I had raped you. Shock came over me when I remember how many times I raped you . . . Mrs. Brown, that word now frightens me to the core when we both know I molested you over and over without your consent over those many years. It was true I saw you as my trophy. Matter of fact, I told you I bragged to the guys on the job about winning the prize. Your pussy is my trophy. Now you have made me face the truth. If anyone knew the truth, they might believe you and arrest me for molestation or even rape. Believe, Mrs. Brown, that was the reason I ignored your cries. Really, I thought you liked it. I have not been taught a lot about a woman's body. Emma, I am learning just like you, even though I am older. There are not enough words to say how sorry I am about your injuries. I told the nurse I would attend the classes on sex addiction. I am going to follow the doctor's orders. We will wait until the baby gets here before we have sex. The therapist had one session with me already. The nurse gave me information. I read it. The brochure taught me that a woman is an independent human being. A woman has the right to say yes or no. No one owns a woman in the United States. This information cites several States laws where a man can go to prison. If he demand or takes sex from a female. It can be your own husband. He can go to jail. It is double as bad if the female is under age. I was so scared after I read this booklet she gave me. I threw the information in the trash can."

Jake dropped his head and said, "I must apologize to you. I didn't know I could still transmit this disease. Living alone without a wife forced me to hook up with a lady of the night. She gave it to me. When she got sick, she told Dr. Jackson I was the person that gave it to her. His office called me and told me to come into his office. I refused. Back in the day, several women said I gave them gonorrhea. When other cases showed up in the community with women I never touched, they found out I was not the carrier. That rumor hurt my reputation.

"Ole Bo's did not like that. It made me mad that Dr. Jackson believed Sally and threatened to turn me into the health department. Earlier that same year, several other girls connected me to an out-spread of venereal diseases. There was no way I would to go into the health department. I am a working man with insurance. I went to my private doctor. My doctor treated me for VD . . . Emma, I thought, I was well. He warned me that repeated episodes of VD could cause me to have trouble fathering a child. You are living proof that I can father a child. Another rumor circulated that there was a second woman that said I gave VD to her. I believe these women gave it to me. This mishap has raised its ugly head again. Young gal, you gave me the best thrill in the world on that special night, so Ole Bo sperms are okay. Let me see what this doctor is talking about. I will go to the desk and ask for the nurse again. It is probably about the schedule for the next session. You said her name was Janet or Dorothy?"

I said, "Yes, sir, her name is Dorothy."

Jake snapped around and rushed to my bed. "Did you tell them anything else? Listen, little girl, you better watch your mouth. I must hurry up and get you out of here." I was trembling as he left the room. Later that night, Nurse Dorothy came to my room. She looked at me and asked, "Are you being abused at home, Mrs. Brown?" I sat up like a big girl and said, "No?" She asked, "Are you afraid of your husband?" I nodded yes. "Has he ever hit you?" I said, "No, please don't get me in trouble. Mr. Brown said he would take care of my baby and me. I have nobody else to help me now. I don't want to talk anymore." I covered my head with my sheet. Nurse Dorothy said, "Please let us help you." The nurse pulled my sheet down and gave me a hug. She said, "Okay, Mrs. Emma Brown, there is help available if you need it. Here is my number. We have help available twenty-four hours a day. God bless you and your baby." She quietly left. I feel safer after her visit.

Jake came to discharge me from the hospital about 10:30 a.m. the next day. Smiling, he said, "Let me get my babies home. Ole Bo is ready to carry my young filly to the house." He was surprised when the doctor walked in. He said, "Mr. Jake Brown, I don't want to see another young woman all mutilated and injured inside from your sexual escapades in this hospital." Jake walked closer to the doctor. "I can't help it I am so blessed down there. Most men are jealous of me, Doc. Maybe some of the doctors are envious of me. You know what I mean, don't you?" Dr. Robinson's face turned red. Jake kept bragging, "My boy will be born soon."

"When Emma delivers our baby, you can help both of us. I don't want you doctors to sew her up as small as you normally do with other women. She needs a larger entrance. Ole Bo must have a bigger gateway." The doctor's ears turned red. He said, "Emma is my patient. We will do what is best for her."

Jake followed the doctor to the door. "Doctor, please leaves a larger space for this rod and all will be well. We know the baby stretches a woman's opening. The doctors usually sew the woman real tight. I don't want her stitch up to tight. Please put that in your notes in case you are not on duty when I bring her in to have my baby. The doctor nodded yes. He said, "Okay, I will work with you to spare this tender young female."

"That is good news for me," Jake said. "You have already seen two other girls that were with me. Trustily I couldn't help myself. I learned my lesson from those encounters. Those females were not my wife. It was hit and go. You know what I mean, Doc. I am sorry I am bigger than most other men. Dr. Robertson, you understand better than anyone how important this is. You can help me avoid tearing my wife any more than I have already. My sweet Emma and I need your help. Leave her opening bigger please. This will help my young tender wife enjoy a happier life. You know I am not going to stop having sex with my Emma. You told me to wait, and I will patiently wait until she delivers. I waited a long time just for her. Ole Jake adores my young wife. We are still newlyweds. You know that it is the duty of a wife to satisfy her husband. Does your wife satisfy you, Dr. Robinson?"

Jake angered the doctor. He said, "Yes, my wife satisfies me very much. I would never injure my wife just for my pleasure." Jake snapped back, "Oh well, there is nothing anybody can do about what I do with my woman. She is my wife. Let's work together to preserve that precious gem of mine." Dr. Robinson was silent for a minute. He said, "I must discuss this with my team. Are you sure you are eighteen years old, Mrs. Brown?"

I sat up and said, "Yes, sir, I am the married eighteen-year-old wife of Mr. Jake Brown. Dr. Robinson said, "Good luck you two. We will see you back when the baby is delivered." Dr. Robinson turned around. He came to my bedside. "Emma, you must go to your regular ob-gyn in three days after this discharge from the hospital. We have already called. You have an appointment Monday morning at ten o'clock. Make sure you are there. If you do not keep this appointment, Social service will come and take you." Jake said, "Oh no, that's my responsibility. I will take Mrs. Emma Brown there on time for her appointment."

Jake drove us home. He said, "I will pay Mrs. Mattie to cook and clean until you get better." My granny stayed with me four weeks. She told Jake to sleep on the couch. I was so happy. I didn't want her to leave. The end of the fourth week, she went home. She agreed to cook and clean until I got better. I was so happy to rest. Now I am eight months pregnant. I was walking around in the house.

I wore big maternity tops around the house. I could only wear panties when I went to see the doctors. My husband did all the washing. One morning, I asked for my panties. Grinning, he said, "I only left one pair of panties out for doctor's visits. I must make sure my little fire box gets plenty of air."

This week I sat and read a lot. My plans are to go back to school as soon as possible. Granny has spoken to several of my teachers that will help me get into adult education. This will be my secret. My husband snapped when I mentioned the idea to him. Now I know I must find a way to go to school while Jake is at work. Jake came home from work. "How are you feeling, big mama?" I said, "Okay." He kissed me and said, "I have been walking around hard so long. I am going to respect the doctor. Granny is gone home, and I got you all along again. The doctor said I couldn't go in your front okay. That is fine. I got a good idea." He picked me up and carried me to the couch. "Mrs. Brown, let's snug up here in the living room. I just want to lie in your lap." He went to sleep and snored. A few hours later, he woke up. "Oh, Mrs. Emma, I am ready to check our little baby out. I want to feel where he is. I am not going to hurt you, my young tender wife."

He kissed and massaged my stomach. This big man was talking baby talk to the baby inside my womb. He said, "I am waiting on you to come on out, little man. You got one more month inside your mama. Okay, you rest, my sweet baby. I got to keep big mama happy while we wait." His head disappeared under my big belly. He said, "My, my, Mrs. Emma's coochie is flaming. It is too hot and the baby needs air." He started kissing my thighs and massaging my vagina. Slowly he began playing inside my vagina. I stiffen up and said, "Quit please. You might hurt the baby."

"No, Mrs. Emma, I am not going to hurt my baby." This slow massage helped me to relax in the chair. Jake enjoyed tantalizing me. Now my body started to respond to his touch. I felt so hot. Something happened. Thrills began to fill my body. Jake peeped up and said, "I see you are enjoying making sweet juice for me, darling

Emma. I got to keep you wanting more. Remember I gave you five great thrills on our wedding night. Okay, relax now, my big baby. This is your biggest bang yet. Warm juice filled the chair. You are wonderful, my sweet rose. Emma, I declare you are sweeter than a Rose. I love your sweet juice."

Jake rested for a while. He lifted me from the chair and carried me to the couch. He turned my body as to facing the wall. Jake slowly kissed my butt. He said, "Don't worry. I will not try to get this entire big rod inside of you, Mrs. Brown. I am going in slow and easy. You must relax and trust me. By law, you are obligated to let Ole Bo get some relief. I don't want to cheat on you with another woman."

I yelled, "You can cheat. It will be okay. Please don't hurt me." I felt that rod pushing against my butt. Jake whispered in my ear, "The doctor can tell me what I can do to the front. He didn't say anything about the back and this big soft butt." He began to massage my butt. Finally he opened my rectum and said, "This hole is so little and pink. It is sweet as a pink rose." The kissing continued for a while. Slowly my husband pushed the end of his rod up into the small round hole. He yelled, "Hold tight, Mrs. Emma. I am going in an inch at a time." He kept grinning and grinning until he finally got the end of his big rod in my butt. I jumped. "Oh, my lord, you are tearing into my butt. Please stop that pain in pure torture. He started laughing. "This butt has gotten bigger since I have been riding in the saddle. You are a high-quality ride, big Emma. Yes sir, you have grown up and filled out a lot in this butt these last eight months. I loved this big soft cushion." Jake pushed a big portion of that hard rod inside my butt. Now inside of my butt, he began to yell, "Get up, girl. Sweet Emma, you got to make it good for ole Bo." I closed my eyes and endured the agony. I had learned from earlier episodes that he won't stop because of my discomfort. This episode went on for a long time. He was so happy when he finally filled me up with his hot lava. He was yelling, "I love it" as I held onto the couch for dear life. This was a different kind of pain and agony that took over my bottom. I cried, "I can't hold on any longer." Jake said, "Okay, turn a loose." I did. He braced me up with his strong hand. "One more ride, I will let you down. I am happy riding inside this big soft butt. This is better than riding in a new car.

"There are no words that can explain this life-changing experience for ole Bo. I just bought a brand new car. Yea, I just drove off the lot with my new ride. I have watched this ride for seven years. I just couldn't wait. Be patient with your husband. It is a rule that a man must train his woman's body to fit him. Men call that a custom design. That is what I am doing now making my custom design ride.

"You better get used to it, Mrs. Emma I got to break this butt in. I never touch your butt or sneaked a ride when I was prepping you. It is tight and right. I love the way it ride. This big baby rides like a chariot. Yes, it firm there is no loose part in this big baby. I will put some salve on it when I get through. I am addicted to this butt. I want this every day.

"I have listen to rich white folk brag about buying luxury cars. Those rides are cherished by their owner. When a white man gets a new luxury car, he wants everybody to see it. I am a working man with a new ride. I want everybody to see my new ride. I mean new bride. We colored folks can't buy a new car. Black men buy used cars but insist on owning a new gal. As an owner, I will smile with pride and say, 'I know you want it, but it is mine all by myself.' Proudly I can park you where everybody can see you. As a new car owner, I will ride with pride. The joy of owning a new car is priceless. Owing you, Mrs. Emma, is worth a million dollars. Yes, my big baby, you are my new car. I mean my new ride.

"I heard ole boss say it can take a while to break a new car in. Nobody told me how long it will take to break in a young hot gal, like my Emma, but we will find out, won't we, gal? A new car has a smell of newness. My, oh, my new ride has that nice smell of a new ride. This smell of you is better than perfume you buy in those high-price stores. Thanks for the best ride ever, Mrs. Brown." Jake carried me to the bathroom and sat me in the tub. Okay, baby, lets soak all of ole Jake out of our lovely butt. Just relax a while." Twenty minutes later, he showered me and dried me off. Smiling, he said, "Let Ole

Jake carry his big present to the bed to rest." We went to bed. Both of us slept until morning. This was a first for Jake.

Granny came to see me. She cooked dinner and left about five o'clock. The three of us ate together. After my granny left, he snuggled up to me. "Last night was the beginning of training that butt of you. Once I get you train to that style of loving, I will be satisfied. This will give your front a rest like the doctor told me. You will have plenty of time to heal after the baby comes. We will get into our routine later. It will go something like this. When I come from work at lunch time, I might want to check the engine to know if any other man been in the engine of my new car. Do you understand?" I dropped my head. I said, "I don't understand."

"Don't worry. We will go slow until you get the routine. After I get off from work, I will come home and take a bath. I must get all those chemicals out my skin. When you get stronger, I want you to cook, then you can put my food on the table. After I eat my dinner, I will watch the news, then it will be time for my young filly and my baby.

"We will put the baby on a schedule. He will come first. Once we get him to sleep, your place is in my bed. A filly knows her place when the cowboy saddle up. The cowboy enjoys the thrill of his ride on his favorite filly. I am going to enjoy riding you Emma, my young filly. Yes sir, Emma, you are my everything. The baby is growing in the front. Last night we found a good substitute as you are budding in my precious soft butt. I got plenty of riding space back there. We will rest a while, then I can ride you maybe two more times tonight. We got plenty of occasions to enjoy even after the baby come out. A baby sleeps a long time in the day. I might trade shift so I can make love while the baby sleeps during the day."

I did not understand all this talk Jake was doing. I was lost in a new world. He continued to give me my new rules of life. "What a ride, what a ride, this is just like riding in a new Mack truck. Come to think about it, you are bigger than most of the woman around here. Yes, you are my new Mack."

I looked at Jake and said, "The doctor came in to see me before I came home. He said my ovaries were bruised and swollen. He said the right ovary is very infected. I told the doctor I didn't understand what happen to my ovaries. The doctor said he remembers you from injuring another patient's ovaries a few years ago."

"Let me tell you, Mrs. Emma, your doctor is mad because he doesn't have the big joy stick I have. Most of the doctors around here know me as the man with the biggest rod in town. When we got married, it was very hard for me. Holding back portion not get it all in. I tried several times. That's how your ovaries got bruised. Maybe I jabbed it too hard." Jake smiled and said, "Big Bo knocked them around trying to get to the promise land." I looked him straight in the eyes and said, "Well, Jake, the doctor said he do not want me to have sex until my ovaries get well. The medicine you picked up from the drug store was for my ovaries." He got up and went into the kitchen, "Did you take the medicine today?" I said, "Yes." "Good, I am glad you did. Make sure you take all of the medicine." Jake came close to my face and said, "Then we are in good shape. The medicine will heal your ovaries. That has nothing to do with my new play place. Ole Bo will be careful playing in the back play pen. My body is now a new indoor playpen for this ole man."

Time stood still for me. I don't know how I got here. Just a little while ago, I was having fun in school. What will my class mates think of me now? I will never have a date with a boy in my age group. I am an innocent child. I am not a teen yet.

I am a twelve-year-old pregnant wife. There are so many words I don't understand. My body is changing right before my very own eyes. I was surprised when my grandma brought me a new training bra size 38C. I love that pretty training bra. That was eight months ago. Why did I need a training bra? What was I training for? Now my favorite bra is too little. Yesterday Jake brought me a size 44DD nursing bra. I was wearing it before Jake got home. He took my clothes off when he brought me to the couch. Smiling at me, he said my clothes were in the way of him checking his baby. My breasts have grown bigger now. Did my breast need training? Why did Jake buy me a nursing bra? Why do I need a nursing bra? What does this mean? What is Ole Bo massaging my breast for? Why do I have to let Jake suck my breast? I am so confused. This was the first year my period started. Now my period stopped. I don't understand any of these grown up things that grandma said I should know. My mama is not here to help me get ready to be a teen.

Now I will never have a girlfriend. I will never go to the prom like my cousins did. All of the things a young girl should experience first. I will never know the joy of the first dance as a teen. Now I can't play on the girls' basketball team. I will never know those feelings. In high school, girls can take Home Economics. I dream of sewing on those big fancy sewing machine. My classmates will march across the stage and receive their diploma. At twelve years old, I have been robbed of this opportunity. I love school. I can't go to that class I wanted to learn literature. There are many great love stories in literature. What a mess this is. Everything has changed because this old man has been playing a game with my future.

How could this happen to me. Now, I am owned by a man that I don't love or like. I can't go to school anymore. There is a rule that a pregnant girl can't go to school with her peers. It can be a bad influence they say. I didn't set out to get pregnant. I don't understand why he did this to me. I did not consent to have sex with this man. As a matter of fact, I thought the word sex was talking about describing gender, if you are a girl or a boy. Jake didn't ask me anything. He tricked me and had sex with me without my permission. I feel so foolish and betrayed. He invaded my body without me knowing it. I know I am an innocent child, raped, molested, and married to her rapist. No one will believe me. The worst thing is no one really cares.

It sickens me to remember all the singing to God Grandma and Jake did. All that singing was just a game for Jake. The singing and jokes served his purpose. Now I wonder when Grandma was supposed to be sleep, was she sleeping? When Grandma went to sleep, Jake kept on singing. He always sang as he rode me on my horsey.

Did Grandma play sleep as Jake rode me on the horsey right out in public? That's the only place I ever rode my horsey. This sneaky man was so doggish that he smiled as he impregnated me out in the wide-open public view. Just like a female dog, I had no control over my ride in his saddle. Jake grinned as he raped me, rocking on my horsey. This brings to mind what I saw one day. I saw two dogs. The female dog ran away from the big male dog at first. The male dog chased her. The male dog caught up with her and jumped up on her back. I remember seeing the male dog take control of the female. He got stuck in this female dog. The female dog was helpless. She was stuck and hollering. She couldn't get away from the male dog. He took what he wanted. I see ole Jake as the male dog that I am stuck to. I can't get away. I am trapped in a house and a marriage. He enjoys riding me like that female dog. Later on that same day, I heard Poppy laughing with his friend. He said, "That bitch dog of mine could not get away from my stud. I rent that big dog out to impregnate other female dogs. Renting a stud out pays well." Poppy bragged. His explanations don't make sense to me. Both male men and male dogs took what they wanted.

The day Mr. Brown married me, he changed his method of taking my body. I was no longer sitting in his lap. Now he is lying on top of me covering me like a big hot blanket. He yells as he rides me. I cannot understand this happening to me now. When I rode my horsey, Jake didn't lay on me, yet he impregnated me. I am still puzzled.

I did not know what was happening to me. I trust Jake because Grandma trusted him. I can't believe she was right there. Oh, maybe Jake put something in her snack to make her drowsy. Thinking back over the last two years Grandma always nodded off after she ate the treat Jake brought her every day.

On the week end when Jake didn't come around, Grandma would sit on the porch and never nodded off. She only went to sleep after she ate her daily treat he brought her. On Friday, he brought her gin. Granny drank her gin and went to sleep. When he finished riding me on my horsey, he would wake up my granny. He always said, "Mrs. Mattie, you better get in the house and go to bed. It is getting late." All I knew was Mr. Brown came five days a week for me to ride the horsey. He always smiled and said, "You need someone to play with, so here I am." Little did I know that my innocent play was used to destroy my future? I didn't understand why I gained weight. I was not eating a lot.

Now my clothes are too tight. Today, I know why my grandma told me I had to live with Jake now. I am captured. My new job is a private maid and sex slave. I saw magazines with stories about sex slave. I did not know what it meant, but I know how it feels to be a sex prisoner now. Why didn't she put Jake in jail for rape? I thought this is America. Negroes don't buy wives. Today, I found that is not true. It has happened to me. I believe this kind of thing has happen to many generations of girls before me . . . Although, I am mad with my grandma for letting this happen to me, I can truly understand what she meant when she told me what happened to her. Now I know how great-granny felt. She told me that when her great-great-grandmother was thirteen years old, a man drove up to the field called the straw boss and asked how much for that chocolate gal over there. Later that evening, the man returned with a cow tied to his wagon. He gave the man the cow and told his young daughter to get on the wagon. She said she never saw her family again.

My great-grandma had the same experience. My great grand-daddy saw her and made a deal with her father. He gave her father a hog and two goats for my great-grandmother. On her wedding night, she found herself along with the man that gave her dad live stock for her. I asked her, "How did it feel to know someone bought you?" She smiled and said, "At least my parent was paid something." On her wedding night, she did not know anything about being alone with a man.

Sex was never talked about with Negro girls. She said, "You just do what the man tells you to do." My grandmother's vagina was bruised and sore. This encounter was so painful she had to stay in bed for two weeks. Home remedies were all they had to use on sore areas.

This old man is now her new husband. He took pride in her tenderness. She was not good at reading, so she didn't like school. From the day she arrived on the farm, she never had any say in the use of her body. It was made very clear to her that her husband owned her body.

Years later, this mother taught her daughters to just let the man go down there and get whatever he wants. "Sometimes he will shoot a boy. Sometimes he will shoot a girl up in you. A man will kill you about what between your legs. He owns your body," the grandma told her great-granddaughter.

"Remember what's between a girl's and a woman legs, belongs to your husband or your man." This young girl gave birth to five children. Her husband had an older woman to catch the babies. This was not a midwife. She was a lady from the church. Grandma said, "You learn on the job. No one train you to make a home. You learn how to be a wife." During this time, women had no rights. Women had no voice. Older women would tell you to learn to obey your man. Many Negro men beat you to let you know they care. Other men beat you to control you. Your environment is controlled, some men choose not to beat their women but control her buying and spending, her friend and family connections.

Beating wives is a common practice in the African-American society. No one will talk about it. Most battered women are told to just forget about the past pain and let sleeping dogs lie. There are salves and ointment used to heal the scars inflicted by husbands and boyfriends. Older women would say, "Just learn how to keep your man happy." "Don't talk back," she said. Granny knows the routine. She has been beaten and battered for many years this seems to be her way to survive.

History has just repeated itself with me. I have been sold to a man by the one person I trust. That one person was my great-grandmother. She was my world. I believed that she loved me and would always protect me. She would never fail me. Granny has let me down. Now I can't do anything about what happened to me.

The cycle of African life continues. Few to none talk about the buying, selling, and trading for young colored girls here in the 50s and 60s. Few books are ever written, discussing this tradition. It is a silent code. No father will discuss this subject. Daughters are never taught about this ritual. They are just a product for exchange. A black girl must abide by the agreement made by her parents or whichever relative she has to live with. The transaction is completed without the girl's knowledge, input or consent. She must go with her new owner in silence.

Now I hate knowing I have been sold without permission. I have no voice. I have no rights as a girl of color. Granny was forced to a make a deal with Jake. I have no control over anything. Four generations of females in our family were traded for something of value. Trading me is like trading a commodity.

My fifth-grade math teacher said, "when you have something of value, you can trade for something you want." She said, "This is called bartering. It is an old system that has been used for centuries. It is alive and well in the African-American society." I guess that was what happened to me. Black Girls and women are commodities or are they?

The years have passed slowly. My body has adjusted to Jake's oversized penis. My mind has adjusted to the sexual demands my husband makes. He has trained and shaped my body so that I now crave the feelings I get when he is inside of me. He works hard at the plant, but he still has enough energy to plunge me into me two or three times a night. He normally rests on Saturday. Sunday, he is much gentler after he comes home from church.

My second baby is a girl. The doctor told Jake to use a condom after I delivered Jake Junior. This would give my body time to heal. When we left the doctor for my last six weeks checkup, Jake began to demand sex without a condom. He said, "That damn doctor cannot tell me what to do with my dick."

Six months later, I am pregnant again. I worked up until my third child was born. This birth is a boy. This is a big task, balancing school, three children, and a mean demanding husband. This will not stop me from going to adult school. Granny keeps my baby three days a week so that I can finish school.

I have one of the best teachers in the world. Mrs. King is a kind spirit with the ability of a genius. I have learned so much from her. My sixteenth birthday found me in the eighth grade. Every assignment I received, I always gave it my all. My grades have remained a B average. I passed all of my classes.

The fear of Jake catching me attending school keeps me scared and cautious. My three teachers have encouraged me to complete high school. Mrs. Jefferson said I will be a great teacher. The doctor says I am two months pregnant again. This baby will be delivered on my sixteenth birthday. What will I do now?

It seems like my husband planned to keep me pregnant so I can't go back to school. Quietly, I said to him, "Why don't you use the condom as the doctor told you to?" He grinned and said, "I can pump as many babies up in you as I want to. Just lay and stay in whatever position I put you in my sizzling chili pepper. I love it, Mrs. Emma Brown."

Time flew by. Mrs. Pitts is my ninth-grade teacher. She picks me up for school. The secretary brings me home. Granny cooks and always has the dinner ready. All is well when Jake gets home. My three children cover for me whenever their daddy asks question about me giving them enough time.

I took my exams for the ninth-grade finals. It surprised me. I am going to do great things when I finish school. Granny is so proud of me. She gave me a twenty-five-dollar saving bond for my birthday present.

This is unbelievable. I am in the ninth grade in adult school. There are several young men in my class trying to get with me. I said,

"No, I don't want to get killed. My husband will shoot both of us." Jimmy is a classmate from elementary school. I always had a crush on him I guess. "This is a full-time job taking care of my home, husband, and four children. I am sorry. This is the wrong time. I wish it was early before I got married."

On the weekend, my children go over to Granny's and stay. She said I need rest. Yes, it is good that I can get rest from the children, but Jake takes advantage of that time. On Friday, he demands three to four hours of every sex act he has seen in his XXX videos and want to try on me . . .

My only concern is my great-granddad Mule. I pray he never try to hurt my baby girl I will kill him if I ever find out he touched her. All my life, I have strived to be a good Christian girl. Now three years later, I have a new friend. She is strong and fearless. Rose has emerged. Her voice is soft and sexy. It is so fun to see Rose lure men and melt them into her spell. She comes forth when I am around a man.

Two nights' straight, Friday and Saturday, Rose came out. She talks to Ole Bo as he got my body ready. On this night, Rose whispered, "You love fucking me in the ass, don't you, my big African warrior?" The old man was shocked. He said, "Look at you, young hot missy. Where did this freaky woman come from?" Jake asked, "Where did you learn to talk like that?" Smiling, Rose said, "You taught me ole pervert, remember? Now I can speak your sexual language. Three and half years of all your hard fucking has made me a woman in control of her coochie. This pussy has a new name. I call it Rose. I remember you saying how you loved the scent of my coochie on your hand. You said it smelled like a sweet rose." Jake smiled and said, "That right, baby. It smell like a sweet rose." It felt good when Rose came out. She was brave and sexy.

My sex life has changed. Jake doesn't control me like he has done in past. Rose chuckled and said, "Ole Bo, you sure know how and when to handle this big dick of yours. Oh, how I love this thick chocolate rod. It feels so good when you shoot that thick hot come in this hot pussy." I quickly realized that Emma is not in control when Rose is having sex. "Listen, big boss man, Rose has been taught by the best. Remember people call you Bo because of your big dick. From this moment, I am Rose with the sweet pussy. I am the woman that can turn your world upside down." Bo stopped and looked down. He asked, "What the hell has happen to you, Emma?" Soft talking, Rose said, "If you want more coochie, you better not call me Emma. Rose is in charge of this coochie." I found myself laughing inside as she yelled, "Lucky Rose is the girl married to the biggest dick in town. Oh, Rose yelled, 'I can't describe how good it makes me feel.' Big Bo has a big long bull's dick. This is better than hooch. I love it. Give it to me, my big stud." After the third round of fucking, Rose whispered, "Big Bo, you can handle this dick like it is a sword. Oh yes, big daddy, you have carved this big soft ass out to fit you. Didn't you say my ass fit that dick like a glove?" Jake grunted, "Yes, hot mama, it is as tight as a leather glove."

Rose reached down and started stroking her pussy. Bo said, "No no, baby, thanks for letting me find an extra thrill." He moved my hand and said, "Oh yes, Ole Bo loves Ms. Rose. I have been waiting to do this to you while I fuck this big ass of mine. Thanks, hot mama. Bo can now put this big hand in this hot hole and fire Ms. Rose's pussy up like a flame burning deep inside." Rose whispered, "I am going to make it good to you, big daddy." It surprised him. "What did you say?" Rose repeated it. She wiggled her butt and asked, "Do you want me to throw this big soft ass to you, big daddy?" He yelled, "Hell, yes." Rose began to move to the rhythm. She whispered, "This soft voice of mine matches this soft ass. You like that, don't you, big daddy? Bo started yelling, "I love it. What the hell happen to my innocent wife?" Smiling, I said, "Jake Brown, you created this whore. That's what you always wanted, wasn't it? Rose will enjoy you tonight. Buckle up, cowboy, let's ride." She said, "You have made a new woman out of Emma."

The truth is, now I like having sex with Mr. Brown. I stay very hot between my legs Many times, I wear him out. One night, he grinned. "I told you once I train that hot pussy of yours, you couldn't get enough of Ole Bo." My husband made sure the doctor stitched me up just right after the birth of each of my children. Having sex with Jake doesn't hurt me like it once did. Now I wish I was with a boy my age. My husband gets tired after a few very hot sessions riding me. To tell the truth, when he gets tired, I am just ready to get it on. Four years of being his sex slave has worn this old man down. Jake can't ride a long time anymore. Now he asks Rose, "Do you enjoy Ole Bo, tantalizing this hot box?" I lie and say, "Yes, sir." Many times, he will smile and say, "You are getting greedy, chili pepper. I work hard, so let me get some rest."

Jake is staying away from home more. He said he is working extra hours so we could get a bigger home now we have three children. My firstborn was named Jacob Jr. My daughter was named for his mother Annie. My baby boy is named Frank. I did not like the name Ann, but I couldn't stop Jake from naming her Ann.

I have a job working at the university to make extra money. I clean the office for a group of history professors. One day Professor Gain asked me if I finished school. I answered, "No, Professor." I was forced to quit in the tenth grade. "Maybe we can help you get your GED." This gave me hope. I told Jake my good news. He grunted, "We'll see. Is my dinner ready?" I smiled and said, "Yes, sir big boss man." "Don't get smart, gal. I will stop you from working over there at the university. The teacher doesn't need to fill your head with big ideas. You ain't no white woman or girl. You are a Negro and the education ain't going to matter. There are very few jobs for colored gals. You got a job here at home taking care of me and these children."

Sadly, I fixed dinner. I looked at my daughter and thought, Ann should have a better life than me. I am going to get me an education. I don't care how long it takes. My baby girl is just four years old. My sons like to play outside. Ann likes to play inside. That keeps me on guard. Whenever Jake calls her to sit on his knee, I tremble . . . I will kill him if I ever see him hurting my baby girl.

One day I said, "You won't hurt Ann, would you, Jake?" He smiled and said, "She ain't old enough for you to worry about that." Jake snapped at me, saying, "I would kill a man if he thought about hurting my daughter." I left the room sad. Now that he is the dad, he will protect his daughter. Who protected me from him?

I heard this ole sick minded husband in the toilet with our son one evening. He was bragging about his big penis. He said, "Jacob, you are big as most grown men. One day, boy, you will be big like me. Then you will be called Bo number two. Oh yea, boy, Daddy will teach you what to do with your wiener." They didn't see me.

I was saddened and felt so hopeless. I went back to school and studied more with the professor. I was able to make good grades.

One Friday, Jake didn't come home. I didn't have a telephone. When he did not come home, it frightened me. I suddenly realized how much I depend on Jake. Saturday came no sign of Jake. Sunday I did not hear or see Jake. Monday he came home. I asked, "What happened? I was worried." He ignored me. We ate supper.

Bedtime came, but Jake didn't ride me. Rose's body got hot when being near him, yearning for his touch. He said he was tired. "I am worn out." Smiling, he said, "Working long hours will wear an old man out."

"Where did you work, Jake? The plant was closed."

"My boss man had me working on his cabin on the lake. It will bring in extra money."

"How many weekends will you be working," I asked.

"Let's get some sleep." The next day everything was okay. The children went to school. I went to work. Jake went to work. The next night, we were all sitting outside. The kids were playing together. It felt so good to know we are secure. My job gave me twenty hours a week. Believe me I save my money. My husband said I could save for the children education.

I took my GED test and failed. It made me sad. Ann said, "Mama, why you are so sad."

"I did not do well on my test for school."

"Okay, Mommy, try again. That's what you tell Jacob and me." We glided through the air in the swing on the porch. All is well. Time seem to fly by. I stopped studying. Jake said, "You know that school is going to get you in trouble. My house better come first. Long as you keep the house clean and keep up with your wifely duty." He called Annie to his side, smiling. "I am happy with my big gal. Look at you. You are tall as I am. Hell, I have to watch you. You might think you can whip me. Don't even think about it. I am in charge. I can tame you, my little filly." He had a smirk grin on his face. It sickens me to know he was watching my baby girl grow up. Now he is calling her a filly, just like he did me when I was her age.

One Sunday morning, we were in church. I noticed a woman rolling her eyes at me. I wondered, What is wrong with this lady? She didn't say anything. One of the ladies of the church, said, "Don't pay her no mind. She just found out her daughter was fooling around with an old man, and it turned out to be the mother's cousin. This man married the little gal a little while later."

"I am sorry about this," I said. I know how that feels . . .

A few weeks later, a man from Jake's job came to the house. He asked me to sit down. "Why?" I asked. "I have something to tell you. Your husband was in a terrible accident. It was fatal."

"Oh, no" I said, "what happened?"

"Well, Mrs. Brown, your husband Jake was riding a young gal, and her husband came home and caught them. He shot Jake dead." My world stopped. I could not believe the man. I thought Jake was working on his second job. I shook my head. I said, "Jake was work-ing on his boss's cabin on the lake. I am sorry, but that can't be my husband. This must be a mistake."

"No, Mrs. Brown, this girl is thirteen years old. Jake once dated the girl's mother. It is rumored that her husband married the girl on her thirteenth birthday a few months ago. The rumor over there is that Jake has been riding that child since she was eleven years old. When this young girl got pregnant, her mother told the young man that he was seen hanging around the house. He was the baby's daddy. Nobody knows the truth. The man married the girl. Both of them are very young. The new young husband left for work. The young man said he knew something was going on when he was at work. That husband only worked a few hours. He doubled back home. This man caught your husband riding his new pregnant wife. The husband stood crying as he pulled the trigger, shooting your husband five times. Jake fell off the child dead when he hit the floor." The man said, "I am sorry to bear such bad news."

When I got myself together, I had to make arrangement for Jake's funeral. I realized I was totally alone with three children without a real job. Thank God my husband had insurance on his job. After the funeral, I started to study again. I took the GED. This time I passed the test.

We developed a new norm in my house. My three children and I now studied together. The children helped me a lot. I continued to work in the university. The people in the community would not let the gossip stop. It was getting too hard to bear. Our family lived in disgrace. We moved ten miles away. I joined a new church. Life was so different. I went to Granny and told her what Jake had said. "How long has your husband been dead?" I said, "Twenty-four months." She did not say anything. She walked out of the room. A few minutes later, Granny came back with a box. She told me to douche in the solution. Smiling, Granny said, "Mule is oversized. He tore me up when we first got married. An elderly church member taught me what to do. Use this six weeks, and your body will shrink. Your female organ can be small as you were a few years ago. Remember you are just a young woman.

There was a casino a hundred miles away. On the weekend, I found myself driving to the casino. I had been winning one out of three nights. One night I won twelve thousand dollars. I stopped when I cashed in my chips. Monday evening, I rushed to the bank and put the money into a saving account. I told the banker, "I want to leave the money in the bank for five years. I need this money to make a profit for my kids." I remembered something Granny said. She said, "Never be greedy when you win. Always leave the casino with your wining." It was six months later before I went back to the casino. One of the ladies from work went with me. We had fun. I played the slot machine and won thirty dollars. We left early. There was a man watching me when I got ready to leave. He walked close to me and said, "Hello, when will you be back?" I said, "Tomorrow night." He smiled and said, "That's good. I want to get to know you." It was nice to have a man interested in me. Rose looked at his package and said, "Maybe you can get to know me."

Saturday evening I went early to the manatee. I played three races and lost. Now I was bored because I lost about one hundred dollars. I thought I have never been to a bar in my life. I strolled into the bar, switching. Slowly I sat down and looked around. There were plenty of men there. I sat on the stool at the end of the bar. I could be seen from all angles. It turned out that Rose was sitting on the bar stool with her legs open and drinking bourbon. This new attention from young handsome men made me stay for the late races. Flirting is fun, Rose thought. I got ready to leave. I headed for the door. Someone walked up behind me. It was a pleasant surprise. He said, "I see you are a woman of your word." We talked for a long time. He asked for my phone number. I smiled and gave it to him. He asked if I was married. I told him my husband was killed. Quietly, he said, "I am sorry." I said, "Wait a minute, I will be right back." I learned to walk differently. Now I swirled my hips as I slowly strode out of the bar. A few whistles followed me in the air. This was so fun. I walked downstairs. I was happy and surprised that the stranger followed me. There were some dark rooms with supplies near the back. I darted inside a room and pulled him in with me. This man was shocked. Quickly, I unzipped his pants. I whispered in his ear, "I saw this in a movie and thought I would try it." Before he could say anything, I slowly stroked his dick with my tongue. He was nervous. I massaged it and sucked hard. He began to grunt. Rose took his load.

The guy asked, "What's your name?" I said Rose. He opened the tie on my wrap-around skirt. It fell to the floor. I was not wearing panties. Quickly I pulled his face down between my legs. This stranger thrilled my coochie two times. I was tingling all over. I said, "Give it to Rose now. I want it. Hell, I need it." He said, "This can't be true. This is tight pussy." I was shocked but happy. Grinning, he said, "Where have you been keeping it?" I whispered, "In storage since my husband was killed." He was a greedy young man. We fucked hard for an hour or more. I heard the announcer say, "This is the last race." I pushed him off me and said, "I must go home to my children." He said, "Can I get your address?" I said no. When I got home, I looked in the mirror and wondered who the person is? The children went to sleep quickly. I sat in the dark and wondered what had Jake created? Could I ever be that innocent girl with dreams again?

My children and I went about our normal routine. On the weekend, the children stayed at Granny. I drove them over to the only home I ever knew. Granny is getting weak and needs their help on Friday, and Saturday. I spent two hours there with them. We had fun.

I came back home took a bath and put on my robe to study. Someone knocked on my door. I opened the front door. Surprise, it was Mule. He said, "Well, well, gal, Ole Poppy has slow walked you down." Clacking his false teeth, he said, "I know the children is not here. I just left them at home with Mattie. I am so glad they are over babysitting your granny. Ole Mule got you to himself. It has been a long time coming. I am so glad Jake is dead. Your crazy husband lost his head for a piece of hot tail. Big Bo is gone and will not be back. You need service, girl." I slapped him. He looked surprised but smiled and said, "That is what I like about you. You got spunk."

Rose said, "Get out you ole pervert. You have done enough harm to the females in this family. I am not afraid of you anymore. This is my damn house. Get out now." I headed for the kitchen to get my knife. He blocked my way. Mule wrestled me down to the floor. I said, "Get up, ole fool." He kept smiling. In a flash, he had pulled my robe open. This time I could not get a way. Mule said, "I waited a long time for this." Old as he was, he was still very strong. This ole goat began sucking my breast. "Oh, yes, he said, "they are better than ever." My bare feet had no effect as I kicked and tried to get up. Struggling, I thought, This man is my great-granddaddy. He should be my protector. Oh no, this selfish ole man is not my defender. He is a horny old sexual pervert. I have studied about them in school. As a matter of fact, I was married to one. It saddens me to remember that this man has changed so many innocent family members' lives. I can't believe he is here in my house trying to hurt me, after all the things he tried to do to me when I was twelve years old. Now I am a woman with his great-grandchildren. He doesn't respect anyone or anything.

Mule was smiling as he rammed his dick in me. He was rocking and moaning. Rose yelled, "What happen to your big dick, old man? Granny said you ripped her open. Well now, you feel like a skinny hot dog to me." Mule stopped. He asked, "What the hell is wrong with you, Emma?" Rose said, "This coochie has a name. I am Rose. If you can't do no more than this, get up." The ole goat said, "Hold on." He said, "I took two red rooster pills before I came over here." He slid off me and began to play in my coochie and suck my fine breast. He said, "This is so fine." Rose said, "You damn right they are fine, ole man." Slowly his dick got hard again. Mule climbed back up on top of me. This time his dick was harder and bigger. He began to yell, "This is the best coochie in the world." Rose laugh and yelled, "You are right. It is certified to be the best in the world. Listen up, ole man, I am in charge. Stop now. The only way you can get your rocks off is you must give me all the money in your wallet or get up and never touch me again. Do you understand?" He pleaded, "Please, please let me finish I will give you anything you want I have waited on this coochie for many years." Rose started wiggling. She moved her body slow and easy. She sped up. He was sweating and yelling, "This is some good coochie." Rose smiled and said, "This is the best coochie you ever had. Rose got pussy power." Ole Mule squirted a small load of come inside of me. It was not a lot. I was glad. I hate this old man. When he finished, he tried to kiss me. I turned my head and said, "Get up and give me all of my money now. Mule got up. He was all weak and shit. Rose didn't care. I knew he carried a few hundred-dollar bills in his wallet. He gave me two crisp hundred-dollar bills. I grabbed the wallet and took all the money. Mule started smiling. "It worth it, Miss Rose, or whoever the hell you want to be." He said, "Do you mean I got to pay you for my pussy? It was mines first. Matter of fact, this was mine before it was Jake." Rose smirked and said, "Oh no, Old slick, Jake got this pussy first while Granny and I was sitting on your front porch. You are an ole cock watcher, Mule." Rose beamed and smirked. "Ha, ha, Jake beat you to this coochie." Mule got mad. "Shut up, gal I tried to fuck you when you were twelve years old on the floor at home and the damn telephone stopped us." Rose said, "You damn right." Poppy came closer to me and started to feel my tits again. I kicked him in the nuts. He bent over and cursed me. He said, "You are a crazy bitch." Rose laughed and said, "You made me a bitch." Rose said, "Get out before I call the police on you and tell them you raped your great-granddaughter." He said, "Ole baby, you would not do that to ole Poppy." Rose laughed and said, "If you don't believe it, stay here in this house another minute and I will show you." Mule slammed the door as he left cussing me. I hated that Rose had changed my life. Emma would be trembling. Now Rose is stronger and not afraid.

This was a horrible afternoon. I showered a long time to remove any trace of dirty ole Mule from my body and mind. I finally settled myself and read my lesson. The next day, I stayed home. That afternoon, the guy I had sex with at the dog track knocked on my door. He said, "Hello, Miss Rose, I am Charles. We met informally before. Now I want to officially meet you." He had a box of candy and flowers in his hand. Smiling, he said, "Ms. Rose, I came to say thanks to you for the best times I have with any woman. When you drove off, I got your tag number. I had a detective friend of mine to track you down for me. I came by yesterday. There was an elderly guy getting out of the car. He said he was your great-granddaddy. I asked, 'Is this Rose's house?' He said, 'No, this is my great-granddaughter Emma's house. She is resting I just came by to console her. She is a poor widower.' I was confused. I believed him and left." Rose smiled and took the gift. Rose said, "That was my great-grandfather. I hate him." Charles said, "I want to get to know you." He studied with me. We went out for dinner and a movie. That Sunday evening, Charles came and studied with me again. He was very smart. He had a master degree in political science. This made going to college classes easier for me. Charles tutored me twice a week. Rose enjoyed the long fucking sessions that followed each college lessons. Charles left exalted each time. Rose loved Charles fucking her for many hot hours. Oh yes, Rose loved it and never wanted him to stop. Charles dated me a year. One day, he came by and told me his job was sending him to Japan. He hoped I would still be around when he returned. I never heard from Charles again. It was like he just fell off the face of the earth

The years were moving fast. My children were growing up before my very eyes. Ann's body developed fast like mine. I stopped my daughter from going over to Granny's house. I knew Mule would try to fuck her if he could. I didn't want to kill Granny's husband. To me, Mule was dead. I hated him. I am in control of my life now.

A year later, my son's basketball coach Levi asked if he could take me and my children to a football game. That night was magical. The week and months that followed brought much-needed joy to our family. We had so much fun. We did many family activities together. My children began to feel comfortable around Levi.

Six months later, Levi took me to his apartment. Rose yearned to have sex. He kissed me passionate. My body was tingling. I wanted him to give me more. Suddenly he said, "We must stop." Rose said, "No no, I need this dick inside of me." He kissed me and said, "No no, we cannot leave the children along too long. We will get back to this later."

We spoke every day on the telephone for several weeks. He said, "I am going to take you on a special date." I was so excited. On that day, Levi carried me to dinner. He took my hand and said, "Well, princess, I have accepted a job in San Diego, California. This is my last week here. I will call you when I get settled." I was so surprised. He left and I never heard from him again. Now I began to wonder what was wrong with me. All the men I got involved with left me.

My children and Granny were my only focus for another year. Granny said, "Take your time. The right man will come along. Your body needs rest after old deceitful Jake." Rose sniggered down inside. If she only knew how many men I have been with since my husband died, it would kill her. Oh well, what she doesn't know can't hurt her. Granny said, "You went through so much with that snake called Jake. The way he deceived me and Mule broke my heart." I dropped my head and said, "I know, Granny. I don't want to think about it any-more." We hugged. I kissed Granny and went home to my children. I was nervous about my second year in college. I buried myself in my books. I made Bs on my final examination. The children were my source of joy. I love them so much.

Two years later, a man delivered my prescriptions from the local pharmacy. He was a short man with a nice smile. "Where is your hus-band?" I said, "He is dead." He said, "I just wanted to know because you are so pretty." I paid him. He turned around and said, "If you ever need help, miss, just give me a call." I closed the door.

Valentine's Day, there was a knock on the door. "Who is it?" He said, "Delivery man. I have a package for you." I open the door. There was a big box of chocolates and a pretty card. Happy Valentine, Mrs. Brown. I closed the door. This simple act made me weak in the knees. I was shocked. I opened the card. There was a fifty-dollar bill inside the card. I was beaming with pride. I placed the card in the middle of the table.

School was out for the summer. I took my children two hun-dred miles away to spend the summer with their uncle and aunt. Alone, I buried my head in my books to study. The first week alone, the doorbell rang. It was the delivery man from the drug store. "I don't mean to intrude on you and your children. I stopped to see if you guys need anything." He said, "I just got off." I smiled and said,

"No, I don't need anything. The children are with relatives for the summer."

"May I come in," he asked. I said yes. "Here is something for you." It was a bucket of Kentucky Fried Chicken and a fifth of vodka. "I hope you will accept this gift. It will let you eat without cooking." I hesitated. "I don't know you that well." "No you don't, but I would like to get to know a woman like you. You are an African queen." We ate and drank. I drank a little vodka. He left like a gentleman.

Three weeks later, a card came in the mail. He invited me to go to a jazz festival. We arrived early at the festival. We met a group of his friends. Everybody was smoking. They said, "Come on, this will make you see life differently." Yes, I did. We smoked much weed. Later we topped it off with crack. Yes, I did crack. Later he took me home. Nothing was the same. This high was like nothing I ever had. My sexual organs went crazy. What is happening to me? This time my feeling was different. It felt like a firecracker went off in my body. I don't remember getting undressed. I found myself in the bed with this short man. He had to be five feet four inches. Here I am six feet two inches tall. I was high as high can be. It felt like magic. Every sex organ inside and outside seemed to be fired up. He was in control of my body. Now this little short man was rocking my world. Every inch of me was sizzling. I was trembling. This was the best sex I ever had. Rose was fired up. He made mad love as he began to thrill me. This time it felt like he appreciated me as a woman. He was nothing like my dead husband. Yes sir, he smiled down at me, saying, "This is the life, making love to a big woman. This feeling makes a man know he is sexy and powerful. Let me take care of you and your children. You have three kids?" I said, "Yes, I do." "Let me help you. If you say yes, you will never have to worry about anything anymore. All I ask is that nobody else makes love to you but me. Think about it, okay." I just lay there, confused. What have I got myself into?

I don't really know this man. Things are moving too fast. He left while I was sleep. He put two hundred dollars in my purse and a pouch of marijuana. How strange is this? I smoked and just relaxed the whole day. The summer was long and hot. That summer, Junior and I went to many house parties. Crack became my easy escape. I really liked the way it made me feel.

Eight months later, I found out I was pregnant. The doctor said I was having twins. I told him the news. Junior's face brightened up like a Christmas tree. This proud dad said, "Everybody calls me Junior. Maybe I will be having a boy that will become my junior."

Junior went to every doctor's appointment with me. He paid for everything. My house was full of everything we needed. He often bragged that "my baby can get anything she wants." I gave birth to twin boys. The proud father played and enjoyed his two baby boys. Some Fridays, he would take the family to the river and fish. We cooked out on the bank of the river. Most nights, we enjoyed the sound of the beautiful waters falling over the dam. There were many times we had fun there until midnight.

A year later, I was pregnant again. I was so big. It was hard to see my feet.

I told him I needed a bigger car. Junior bought me a van. Then, I was the mother of seven. Life is busy. My granny's family adores my children. Everything is going good. Both set of twins were born with some mental deficiencies because both parents were smoking crack. The babies were delivered without any problem. We celebrated the new addition to the family. Sometime on the weekend, Junior said, "You need to get away and have some fun." He paid my two cousins to babysit.

We partied for two days in Atlanta. Junior was able to keep his job even though he was smoking crack. His boss really liked him. One day, his boss said, "Boy, you are getting very skinny. We are going to send you to get some help. That night, it didn't matter. We smoked and made much mad love. He said, "Baby, this is the best night of my life I am truly happy. I am enjoying this high so much. What about you?" Rose said, "This pussy is sizzling." "Okay, Ms. Rose, I am going to make our fire hotter. Smiling, he said, "I am going to double up so we can go flying a little bite higher. After he doubled up, he was yelling and laughing. We were having crazy sex. Then he began to slow down. He sounded different. He was huffing and puffing. Suddenly he fell off me. He didn't respond. I tried to wake him up. I panicked and called 911. They took him straight to the hospital. They rushed him to intensive care. I went to see him. There was a young lady that looked just like Junior. I said hello. I asked her, "Are you Junior's sister?" She said, "No, I am his daughter." I was shocked. Just then another woman stepped in the room. She said you must be his bitch. How many little bastards do you have with Junior?" "Mrs. Lady, I don't know who you are, but my kids were conceived in love. Junior takes very good care of his family. I have four children with him. I don't want any mess. I just want to know how Junior is doing." The daughter grabbed me by my hair and started to beat me. I was fighting for my life. I knocked the mama down. The security guard had to pull them off me. There were scratches and bruises all over me. The daughter tried to cut me with a knife. I beat ass for a while. I lost it. All I could think about was why were those fools beating me?

The woman said, "Junior is my husband. We have been married for twenty years." The next day, Junior died. The hospital and the police were talking about charging me with manslaughter after the wife told them I gave Junior the crack. That was a lie. Junior always brought the crack. I don't know where he got it from. To tell you the truth I did not know Junior's official name until I saw it in the newspaper. There was a nice picture of him followed by a short obituary. It was a shock for me to find out that my children's father led a double life. The man was a skillful liar. There were no signs of deceit while he was with us. Our children loved their father. Now I have to face reality. It all was a lie. There was a note in the newspaper obituary section that gave his age. I was devastated. He was old enough to be my daddy. His wife was a woman the age of my mother. I am astonished it can't be real.

There were many threats made by Junior's wife and family. They found my grandmother and left threats there. After this was over, I had to move for our safety.

The night before the funeral, I went to the funeral home. One of the funeral home staff knew me from birth. He knew my grandmother. He was kind enough to give me a program. He did not know I was the other woman. He just knew me from my childhood. I wanted to attend his funeral, but that was impossible. I was miserable and lost. I had to go and said my good-bye to him. I kissed Junior on the forehead. I told him, "I love you very much." I also told him his children loved him and will miss him. My prince charming was gone never to return again. Emptiness hallowed my life like never before. How did this happen to me. I was trapped and so abused by my first husband. Now my lover has deceived me.

Thinking back, I remembered how Junior entered my life. It felt like my prince charming had arrived. The man was the opposite of Jake. Junior brought love and tenderness into my life. There was a level of respect I had never experienced before with my parents, great-grandparents, or Jake. Now Junior is gone.

It feels like I am walking in a bad dream. I wanted to wake up and find out the nightmare is not real. I kept saying, "Please, God, let this be a bad dream. How could this be real? Five days ago, Junior was making sweet love to me. That night his voice rang out as he yelled baby, we are flying. It is so much fun. He said I love you sweet Rose. Junior seemed so happy on our last night that night." In a quick flash, everything changed. He died and left me.

I brought the program home. On that night, it took courage and strength to face my children and tell them that their daddy was dead. I told them, "Daddy would never come around again. They took it very hard." This loving and supportive father spent a lot of time with our children and me. We took trips together as a family. I don't know what he told his wife to be away from home, but he gave us a good life.

My children and I held our own memorial service for Junior at the park. We wore black shirts. At the end of the ceremony, we released balloons in his memory. This was one of the saddest days of my life. Now I have seven children and both of their fathers are dead.

Reality slapped me in the face. I got in the van and cried as I remembered how Junior grinned when he hand me this special gift. He gave me a box. Inside the gift box were the keys to the van. It was a surprise gift when I was pregnant. Yes, it was two years ago. He lavished many gifts upon me. Junior bought the van so we would have enough room to ride together. The first week after he bought the van, he said we were going on a family trip. We were gone for four days on that trip.

The man was at our house three to four days a week. He said he lived with his elderly parents and didn't want to stay overnight at our house. We all thought he was just dedicated to his older parents. Now I know that was a lie. It is a must that I check the title on my van.

The next week, I called the dealership where he purchased the van. The car dealership manager called me back and said Junior's name was on the first line as the buyer. My name was on the second line. He said, "Come in." When I arrived, the manager invited me in his office. He said, "I am sorry about your loss. The good news is the van is now yours." The insurance on the van paid off the balance. He gave me the title to the van and told me the balance was paid off. "Our Company had the title changed to your name. Today this van is officially yours. After the pay off we present to you a check for $1000. We hope this will help you and Junior's children." Tears washed my face.

There was a lot of anger deep down inside of me. I felt sadness and pain as I walked out of the car dealership. Reality is here. I am alone with seven fatherless children. Both dads are dead and gone. On this day, I vowed to protect my daughters from sexual predators.

My new mission in life is to teach my girls that they have a great protector and leader. I will lead and guide them from this day forward. I will teach my sons how to be honorable and honest. Most of all, I am going to teach my sons that a girl and a woman are precious. My sons will know that a woman has rights. When she says no, that means no. I want to teach them the importance of a female in society.

Only a female can bring life into this world. I will drill it over and over that the female should be cherished. I don't want them to ever take advantage of a female. This cycle of abnormal behavior must end here. When this is all over, I am going to get counseling for all my children and myself.

I got a call from Junior's employer. He asked if there was anything he could do to help me. I said, "I am alone now with his four children and three children from my marriage. My income is very little." The manager helped me get a death certificate. The company filed for the insurance. He wrote a letter stating that Junior had my four children on his company insurance. Six weeks later, I received a check for ten thousand dollars. The drugstore owner said Junior's other children with his wife was older and couldn't receive the money.

I packed our van and left for a new start. I heard about New Orleans, Louisiana. We sang and enjoyed the trip to the magical city. We found a nice house. The weather was nice. The children fell in love with our trips to the Gulf of Mexico. My oldest son was a good fisherman. We went fishing three times a month. Time went on and we adjusted well. I did not like being alone. The loneliness became overwhelming.

My children found contentment there. I got them all in school. My goal became very clear. My seven children were the center of my life. The board of education gave me a job as a janitor. Now I had great benefits to protect me and my family. My new employer told me I could apply for a teacher's position as soon as I finish my last year of college.

It has been five years since Junior passed. Life was hard with all the children. Finally, a social worker at school asked me about their dad. I told her he was dead. She asked, "Did they receive any benefits from him?" I said no. I dropped my head in shame and said, "He had a wife. I did not know this until the day before he died in the hospital." The social worker smiled and said, "We can't change the facts of our life, but we can change the way we chose to live it. Take these papers with you and fill them out. I will help you get assistance for these children . . ." It took a minute to find all of their birth certificates. Each child's birth certificate had Junior's name on it. We filed for assistances. My children were able to receive dependent benefits from their dad. New Orleans was a nice place. I needed to leave my past behind me.

A few years later, I met a quiet man that stole my heart. After dating me for two years, he asked me to marry. We got married. He moved us into a bigger house. My husband Sam is a hardworking man. We have two children together. He has four children by a previous marriage. Together, we have thirteen children.

My oldest son has mood swings now. The doctor gave him medicine. Most times, he is very quiet and withdrawn. He had a difficult time in school. Finally, a class caught his interest. He began to draw. He now designs art on the computer. His grades improved. The counselor said my son should take a certificate of completion. His teachers have given him a social pass because he never missed school. He marched with his class and received his certificate. He was disappointed but never said anything until after graduation.

He enrolled in the twelfth grade in another school. He went back in the twelfth grade and passed all his classes with a 3.0 average. This young man defied the odds. "I can read and comprehend, Mama," he said. "I am going to let the teachers know I can learn." His former principal and teachers said they assumed he was special because of his parents' drug abuse. Therefore, they never gave him the same work as other kids. The following June he marched across the stage and received his diploma.

My mission is to teach my daughters about their bodies. We are a part of a support group. This helps me explain to my girls their importance as human beings in America. They need to know that they are valuable human beings. Most of all, I want the girls to know they are not property. Each girl has rights. Every female is the boss of their body. There will never be anyone in our lives that will be able to manipulate us as Jake did Grandma and me.

We watched a documentary on kids in sex trafficking. Later on, we were on our way home. My daughter asked me, "Are there predators living among us?" I said, "Yes, sadly there are. Your mother will be hyper vigilant with you guys. I will look out for special friendships. This can be used to lure children into their trust. I will be watchful and truthful to my children. I understand that you are young now, but predators start watching you when you are very innocent and naive. I knew I became a victim of a sexual predator. He was a child molester dissykies as a friend. In his sick mind he was fascinated with innocent children."

Believe me I do not want anyone of my children to become a victim like I was. My life would be so different now if I had someone to protect me when I was a child. I will guard all of my children.

Most of all, I will teach them about their rights as children. I am working very hard to establish truthful relationships with my children about monsters that live among us. All seven of my children are in therapy now.

Finally, I have three years of higher education. I can teach the basic principles of life to our girls. Education is the key to be able to read, write, and comprehend.

We love living in historical New Orleans. This place has a big group of retired seniors. There are many senior volunteers here where I work. I was surprised to hear the men talking about money-hungry American women. Three of them bragged they had mail-order brides. I know that one was an Italian engineer that recently divorced his white wife. He said, "She took almost everything I owned." This turned my heart into stone. "The American dream sucks when it goes wrong," he said.

Now my new neighbor brags that he has a Russian girl. "I ordered her through a magazine. All she asked for is a credit card she can shop with. I gave her a card with a $1,000 limit. She never spends over $500 or $600 a month. She is very obedient. This is a bonus. She gives me great sex too. My prenuptial gives her nothing. She will get $5,000 at my death. I plan to live a long time." He smiled and walked off. He is a friendly reminder of the men in my past.

Ann is my oldest daughter. She has changed since we moved here. We have three young cousins visiting us from Detroit, Michigan. One asked me why I was going to the doctor. I said, "I am going to therapy." She said, "I don't know what that is. Can I catch anything from you?" I smiled and said, "No, I don't have a disease. My doctor is a psychiatrist. He is a medical doctor that assesses and treats mental health disorder. My psychologist is also a doctor. He offers me psychological treatments called talk therapy. It takes time to get over or get past certain emotional problems I have since I was a child. I need all the help I can get."

Ann smirked and said, "My mother has all of us going to therapy. I hate it. Most of all, I don't need it." A few days later, the therapist talked to me and said. Ann is not focusing on the treatment we have developed for her. Maybe she will come around. This young lady has a mind of her own. Her values sometimes frighten me. We will not give up on her. Maybe this is just a phase of adjustment. She began to act out at the oddest time. I told her she could ask me any question about her father and me if she wanted to. She smiled and said, "I am good."

I asked Ann to be nice on the special date. Sam took us to the French Quarters. The food was so different. The Cajun taste is better than good. The children loved the food especially the beignets. We came home and got the children all in bed. Sam and I went out on a date.

Life is so good for me and my family now. Sam is a dedicated father. I have told him about my past. He said, "I am glad that we came straight about our past before we got married. I have a checkered past also. It helps to face your faults and work to correct your problems. These children are depending on us to provide a wholesome home for them. This is what we will do."

Sam said, "My wife and I were two functioning alcoholics. A few years ago, she got sick and died from cirrhosis of the liver. That was a wakeup call. I got help for myself from the doctor. Today the after effect from my cirrhosis shows up in my high blood pressure. You know I eat healthy now. I will never mistreat my body again. The church is the place I draw strength from. It helps me also to stay connected to alcoholic anonymous. This support system has been great in connecting me to others that are still in addiction. Thank God I am out of addiction and enjoy a normal life with you and our children. This felt good to know we are okay."

A few days later, Denise, the ten-year-old cousin that was visiting us was crying. I asked what the problem was. She said, "I can't tell you." "Why?" I asked. Denise said, "Ann told me she would kill my baby sister if I told anyone our secret." That shocked me. I wrapped my arms around her and said, "I won't tell, okay?" She whispered, "Ann sneaked in my bed and kissed me. It scared me. I told Ann I never let anybody kiss me but my mother and father. Ann said, 'This is a different kind of kiss I will teach you.' She started rubbing my vagina. She whispered, 'We are going to have fun.'

"Ann whispered, 'I watch my mama play with this toy. She likes this toy so well that she holler when she stick it in her. My mother never sees me peeping and watching her.' Ann said, 'I tried playing with this toy and love the way it makes me feel. It is fun to watch and play with.' Ann said she saw Sam your husband playing with you and this toy." Denise held me tight. She said, "You promise." I said, "I promise." Denise said, "I told her to stop. She slapped me. Ann said this was your special toy. She was going to let me see how it feels." She said, "Ann was kissing me between my legs. I was kicking. I slapped her. Cousin, your daughter Ann smiled and said, 'Trust me you are going to love the way this toy make you feel.' Then she turned the toy on and pushed it in my vagina. It was frightening, as Ann pushed your toy in my vagina. I screamed. Ann hopped up and ran. I am scared, cousin. I called my parents. They are on their way down here now." My whole world flipped. Quickly, I carried the frightened child to my room. I called her parents. They were so angry. My cousin Maggie said her husband said he was going to kill Ann for touching his child. We never imaged such thing would happen to a child. The angry mother said, "We will be there in another twelve hours." Frantically, I called Ann into the kitchen. I asked, "What in the world did you do to Denise?" She smirked and said, "What you are talking about?" I said, "You have violated this child. How could you do this?" Ann smirked and said, "She is a liar." She ran to her room.

A knock on the front door frightened me. I answered the door. There were two policemen at my door. The officers said, "We received a call from Detroit today the parent had a warrant sworn out for Ann's arrest. They requested our local precinct to pick her up and detain her until the parents arrive." The police asked for Ann Brown. I called her. She didn't come. The policewoman asked what room does she sleep in. I pointed her to Ann's room. She was nowhere to be found.

The officer asked Denise to come with them to the hospital. The female officer said, 'We will have someone to protect you until your parents arrive. You can't stay in this house another hour." It felt like a ton of bricks had hit me in the face. I was walking around in a trance. They searched the house and the yard. Ann was gone. I sat there astonished. How could this happen. Why did this happen.

Denise's parents arrived. I told them the police had already taken Denise to the hospital. Maggie was yelling at me. She asked, "How could you let this happen to my helpless child?" That was the last time I saw my cousin.

Twenty-four hours later, the neighbor said they saw Ann under the bridge. Mrs. Green said, "I called her and asked was she okay? She said, 'Yes, I am good,' and then she ran off. The next day, I got a call from the jail house. They found and arrested Ann for molesting a child.

All the help I have sought and given my daughter Ann has not helped her. She seemed to have deviant thoughts in her mind. This is the wrong time for this tragedy to happen. I am graduating from college in two weeks.

About the Author

The author lives in North Carolina with her family. She has two other books published.